WHY
I FIGHT

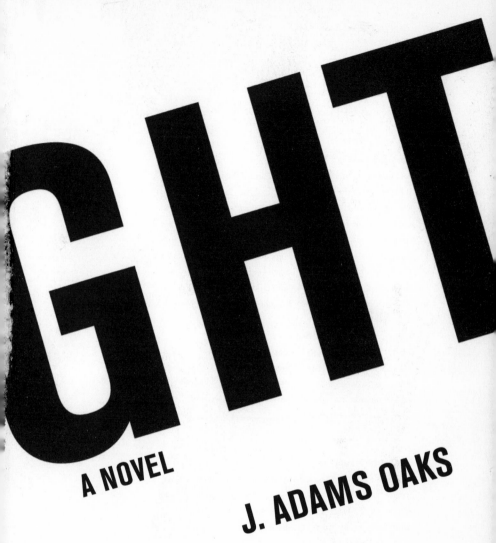

GHT

A NOVEL

J. ADAMS OAKS

A Richard Jackson Book
Atheneum Books for Young Readers
NEW YORK   LONDON   TORONTO   SYDNEY

Atheneum Books for Young Readers

An imprint of Simon & Schuster Children's Publishing Division

1230 Avenue of the Americas, New York, New York 10020

This book is a work of fiction. Any references to historical events, real people, or real locales are used fictitiously. Other names, characters, places, and incidents are products of the author's imagination, and any resemblance to actual events or locales or persons, living or dead, is entirely coincidental.

Book design by Mike Rosamilia

The text for this book is set in Filosofia.

Manufactured in the United States of America

10 9 8 7 6 5 4 3

Library of Congress Cataloging-in-Publication Data

Oaks, J. Adams (Jeffrey Adams)

Why I fight / J. Adams Oaks.

p. cm.

"A Richard Jackson book."

Summary: After his house burns down, twelve-year-old Wyatt Reaves takes off with his uncle, and the two of them drive from town to town for six years, earning money mostly by fighting, until Wyatt finally confronts his parents one last time.

ISBN-13: 978-1-4169-1177-7

ISBN-10: 1-4169-1177-4

[1. Uncles—Fiction. 2. Fighting (Psychology)—Fiction.
3. Emotional problems—Fiction. 4. Criminals—Fiction.] I. Title.

PZ7.O1052Wh 2009

[Fic]—dc22

2007046433

To my family, for their love and support

Thanks to: my editor, Dick Jackson, for his caring, brilliant guidance; my agent, Barbara Markowitz, for her faith in my work; Matthew Smith, for pointing me toward Barbara; Randy Albers and the Fiction Writing Department at Columbia College; Claire Fallon and Steve Kalinosky, for getting me on track; Kim Morris and Megan Stielstra, for keeping me on track; and a small group of spiders, for helping me start this adventure.

WHY
I FIGHT

CHAPTER ONE

DON'T CALL ME KIDDO.

I REALLY hate it. People been calling me that way too long. Fever and Ma and Uncle Spade all call me kiddo, and it makes me crazy. See how I ain't smiling? People who know me, know that means trouble. Oh man. Look at me, all wet and shaking and messed up—JEEZ, and blood on my fist. I ain't a good guy. Even my own ma says that. I just left her and Fever again, but I ain't never going back.

Gosh, my knuckles hurt. Look, I can't barely make a fist. I'm used to the pain, but this hurts different. I been bare-fist fighting a long time now and I know how to keep from busting my bones or shattering my wrist. Learned the hard way. I've cracked a bunch of ribs and fractured my eye socket in a few spots. Can't count how many times my nose has been snapped.

But believe me, I done some damage too, sent guys to the hospital a bunch. I was real good at winning. So what I'm saying is, I don't care that my fist hurts. What's peeving me is this dried blood on my knuckles. Listen, soon I'm going to need some ice for this swelling.

See, Fever and me, we'd got this parking lot together. We planned it and bought it and built it together, him and me. Used most of my leftover fight money. It was a big deal, us two working together after me being away almost six years. And tonight was opening night, but junk went wrong. This is Fever's blood on my knuckles. He got me so peeved I popped him in the face. I usually got better control than that. I gotta calm down now. Take a deep breath.

What happened was, back on my twelve-and-a-half birthday, we was suddenly homeless and got put in the Downtown City Shelter. I didn't got no shoes and my feet were real cold and real dirty, so this super-nice social-worker lady, she tried to find me sneakers that'd fit, which ain't easy. Me being already six foot tall with my feet as big then as they are now. I rubbed them while I waited, locked in that old lady's office, listening to Ma stomp around outside the door and wail about how she wanted to kill herself. Fever hollered too. Pounded on the door, saying, I KNOW YOU'RE IN THERE, WYATT! Made me smile, knowing they were finally thinking about me. Fever hollered at all the city workers how he wanted to kill me.

2

Those workers gave them both pills to quiet down, then put them in locked rooms. Later, even though I still didn't got no shoes, I took some of those pills too. And when I woke up, there my uncle was, kneeling by my cot, whispering:

—Come on, kiddo, let's get you out of here. You're coming with me.

CHAPTER TWO

MY UNCLE SPADE, HE
was the one guy who made my world seem special. He was like a parade. Back when I was little, when we still had a house, he'd suddenly be there, busting through my folks' door, flipping on lights, cranking up the hi-fi, tossing bottles of booze and decks of cards on the table, talking so loud Ma'd holler at him to shut up. He'd spin me around almost like a hug, then send me out to his car to grab gifts he'd brung from all over—maps and wigs and combs and caps and candy. He'd make Fever play cards till morning, me sleeping by their feet on the floor, waking in time to see him sneak out like Santa Claus. Jeez, back then you'd have thought he was the best thing in the world.

So leaving the shelter with him was exciting. He swooped me into his shiny white rumbling Chevy, and I listened to every word he said. I remember hoping my mustache would grow in as dark and smooth as his. I wanted to get a tattoo and swig back beers and whiskeys and cup a ladyfriend in my arm easy as a sack of groceries. I was such a idiot. I didn't get none of who I was. I was nobody. I was a scrawny, pale, scared, empty, bumbling kid. Jeez, I used to watch his every move. Copy him. Think I could handle a Lucky Strike, pretending to smoke a toothpick.

Surprised me how easy it was to forget Ma and Fever the way we raced down the highway, windows open, that old life spilling away from me. No more school. No more stinky jeans. No more fixing my own food. No more being alone in that dark, damp house. Before they lost it. Them two was never around (always had a job or a second job or beers that needed drinking), and that place was so quiet and empty even my hollering meant nothing. Then suddenly I had somebody who'd listen to me (or pretend at least). Somebody who'd buy me things, drag me along with him everywhere he went, and introduce me to all kinds of folks. That was being loved, wasn't it?

I'd never been traveling before and so everything we did was like . . . vacation. And what kid wouldn't want to be on a vacation all the time? I woke up when I wanted, ate what I wanted, and played all day.

That first night in the Chevy, Uncle Spade shook my foot, said he needed smokes. I dragged myself out of the car, the cold air waking me. There stood this giganto truck stop, like Las Vegas it was lit up so beautiful. WOW. Flashing lottery signs, white semis with custom-painted cabs covered in ladies and flames and glitter, that smell of gas and open fields and fried food. Like magic. You only get to see something for the first time once.

Inside, I wandered the aisles barefoot. My uncle hollered to me while he filled himself a soda from the machine.

—GET YOURSELF WHAT YOU WANT, KIDDO, AND SEE IF THEY GOT SHOES.

I couldn't hardly stand it and I couldn't stop smiling. Get myself what I want? When could I ever do that before? I didn't never have money, and I didn't never just pick stuff at a store. So I thought real careful about it. I still remember exactly what I got: one extra-large grape soda, a chocolate bar, a cherry sucker, a bag of extra-cheesy tortilla chips, and a pair of red and white flip-flops (since they didn't got no shoes). Uncle Spade, he didn't even blink. He paid with a hundred, saying nothing, like people just buy what they want and carry hundred-dollar bills in their pockets to spend all the time. I grinned like crazy, climbing back in the Chevy, not sleeping for a long time, afraid I'd make a mess. Took me a long time to learn how not to be such a scaredy-cat.

CHAPTER THREE

WHEN I WOKE UP, WE
were pulling down a long, dusty driveway. Uncle Spade didn't tell me where we was. He never bothered telling much if he didn't have to. He'd just pull his big old Chevy over and tell me to hop out. He'd stuff his pack of smokes in his pocket, smooth down his mustache, and start walking. Could have been a motel or a carnival or a ladyfriend's house. That morning I didn't know whose weedy yard full of rusted cars and farm tools we was in. Asked him about it, but he just pretended he didn't hear nothing, stretched his legs, and wiped the sweat off his forehead. My heart was racing pretty good. Problem was, I'd never really been anywhere before or talked to many people.

We stepped up on that porch and heard screeching, like a cat getting its tail pulled, and man, my heart beat faster. When the screen door slammed behind us, first thing me and Uncle Spade saw was a little old lady leaning her cheek up against the side of this super-tall clock. Spade called out:

—MA?

And boy, that made me peeved, finding out I'm seeing my own nana. His holler made her jump, that clock swaying. She spun around, squinting toward his shout, a copper key on a leather cord swinging around her neck. Her eyes looked full of lard. I didn't remember her too good from before, but she was my nana. I must've been only six, maybe seven, when Fever and Ma brought me to that house 'cause my grandpa'd died. I remembered Nana was already shrunk and had the hump, but she looked more like Fever and Spade back then. Now she just looked shriveled. What I didn't remember was the stink of the place or the living room stacked with crates of broke glass or the piles of cats laying around.

So how come he didn't prepare me a little, maybe warn me she's going to act like a crazy witch? I got mixed up inside with mad and scared and confused. And it wouldn't be the last time. I just had to get used to Uncle Spade not caring what I thought.

—HOW THE HECK DID YOU GET IN HERE? Nana shouted, not 'cause she was deaf, but 'cause she was real peeved. A bunch of the cats glared at her and scurried out the back door.

Spade told her the door'd been wide open. He smoothed

down his hair, so I smoothed mine down too and made myself smile, but she just kept shouting:

—WHO ARE YOU?

She closed her left eye, moving her head around to get a sight of us.

—Ma? What the heck are you doing, Crazy Lady?

—Walter? That you?

—No, Ma, he explained. Your other son. What are you doing? Hiding? You get stuck?

Walter is Fever, who's my dad. I call him Fever 'cause when I was little I couldn't say father and Dad never fit. And my uncle, he's really Franklin, but only his ma and one of his ladyfriends is allowed to call him that. He's Spade 'cause of the farm. As a kid, my uncle got his nickname for using a spade to kill mice and stuff. He'd swing one so quick, he'd take off a muskrat's head before it knew it got hit. In the City, people took his nickname as a challenge to beat him at poker. Only a few real stupid guys made the mistake of thinking the nickname came from his thick, curly black hair. They'd joke about it, and his spade-swinging hand'd raise up quick and crack a nose for the comment.

Nana jutted her head out like a bird.

—I'm moving the dang thing, she said, so I can read him in the light and wind him up. And SHOOT, I can move him any way I want, YOU HEAR ME?

Only Nana said the cuss words I won't say, ones old ladies shouldn't use in front of their grandsons. She probably didn't recognize me, since I'd grown so big I had to duck under the doorjamb when I walked in. Nana asked who else was there, her head bobbing again till she aimed her better eye at me. I just hung back, shaking and grinning like a idiot and trying not to smell the cat stink. Uncle Spade explained I was Walter's boy, Wyatt, didn't she remember?

Nana nodded, thinking, saying sure she remembered, then turned her back to us. She opened the clock's belly and reached between some weights and chains. With the string still around her neck, Nana used that copper key. Springs tightened inside, filling the room with this creepy sound like metal hangers in a empty closet. More cats skittered off. I asked my uncle what was wrong with her, and he whispered how she'd lost her marbles, but I didn't know what that meant.

—She's loony, I'm telling you, Spade explained. Just look . . . it's summer, for Christ's sake, and she's still got a freaking wreath.

He was right. One hung off the banister, needles crunching under our feet. Nana shut the clock, bent down, and shoved a crate out of her way. Each one was full of a different colored glass, broke brown bottles and broke white plates and broke green glasses. Then she stood on her tiptoes, facing the clock, peering up, looking like she was waiting for a kiss.

—Ma, it's seven a.m. . . . . MA! YOU HEAR ME? I'm telling you the time.

—I can dang well see the time. It's seven-oh-three, RUDE SON.

She shuffled around more crates and Uncle Spade stepped into the room, kicking a black cat out of his way. She touched the front of his sweaty T-shirt with her crooked fingers like she was checking if he was real. That was all either of us got. The only hugs I remember getting was from Miss Paz, my third-grade teacher. I always waited by the door after class to say good-bye, hoping she'd reach down and put her arms around me.

Nana pushed Spade aside and waved me closer. Like with the clock, she leaned up and squinted her eyes at me, grabbing hold of my face. She pulled me down till her hot breath hit my cheek, smelling like onions and coffee. I held my breath, us getting eye to eye. Hers were yellow like the lace curtains. She seemed to be part of the house, skin puckered and spotted like the wallpaper. Even her fuzzy hair looked like cat fur.

—Jesus. You look like Walter, but you're bigger. So big. Just like your papu. But more handsome than any of them. Wyatt? You're Wyatt, then? Huh . . . , she said, and thought about my name a bit before letting go of my face. Big as the granddad you was named after.

I liked that, even if he was dead.

Spade and me sat at her rickety, burn-marked kitchen table

while Nana made coffee. She had trouble finding everything and I wanted to help, but I was still scared of her. Besides, them two kept mumbling a conversation with no break. Uncle Spade told her stories about good jobs and good pay. All of them made up. So I just sat there, practicing politeness.

That night, Uncle Spade slept in his old bedroom—the one him and Fever had shared. He stuck me in the big, open attic. There wasn't no space for me to lay down on the crate-covered floor downstairs. Besides, the cats freaked me out. At Fever and Ma's, I'd stopped sleeping in my bed a couple years before, once my ankles started sticking over the footboard. I sat on the mattress to do homework and dragged my pillow to the rug for sleep. So that night I lay on a pile of fuzzy blankets and watched spiderwebs sway from the roof beams, listening to bugs singing outside, the house creaking, tree branches scraping. . . . The last thing I remember before I fell asleep was thinking how it was too quiet and too noisy at the same time.

CHAPTER FOUR

THE NEXT MORNING I
jumped awake to the sound of Uncle Spade kicking more
cats and banging out the front door. He started up the Chevy
and my heart ran fast. I could've swore he was leaving me. It
all made sense—him and Fever'd made some secret plan to
ditch me with the old lady, of course. He was probably sick of
listening to me.

I scrambled over a basket of yarn and swiped a rack of deer
horns out of my way to stumble down the dark back stairs. I ran
my hands along the walls, my bare feet thumping all the way,
then busted through the kitchen and out onto the back porch in
my underpants, stubbing my big toe on something that rolled
down the steps and broke like glass on the hard dirt. Nana's
whole yard was all dry and cracked like her knuckles.

—UNCLE SPADE, I shouted. WAIT!

The car was there. He'd backed around near a metal shed by a old rotted tree stump. When he turned his head to hear me over the engine growl, the car choked and died. He started cussing, but that was okay. At least I'd stopped him.

—UNCLE SPADE! WHERE'RE YOU GOING?

My toe stung like a bee bite, throbbing all the way up into my head. I leaned my elbows on my knees to catch my breath. Leaning down, I could see what I'd kicked. It was one of those plaster elf kind of things with a red hat and white beard, his round belly broke open.

—Dang, I muttered.

—What's up your butt, Wyatt? Chill out and stop breaking things.

—Where you going?

He leaned out his window, grabbing a piece of the door.

—I'm gonna drag that junk washer from the front yard into the ditch back here. Crazy naked kid, get some freaking clothes on so you don't scare your nana. And then get out here to help me, will you?

—Yeah, sure, I said, turning red for all my skin showing.

I stood up, covering my parts with my fists, and took a step down to see if I could fix that elf. As I picked up his head, I noticed a whole pack of eyes watching me from under the porch—creepy cat eyes mixed with more of them goblins holding tools and pushing wheelbarrows, all of them looking past the dead one to me. I shivered and shoved the broke pieces under there with the others.

—Wyatt, what the bleep are you doing? You gone loony as your nana? Haul it upstairs and get dressed, Uncle Spade said, starting the engine.

When I came back down, Nana's bottom jutted out the refrigerator, her head stuck way inside. She was getting her good eye close to the foods, and once she found what she wanted, she backed herself out with a big clear-glass bottle of milk, which she opened up and sniffed.

—Don't worry about breaking my elf, Nana told me.

I nodded, relieved. A greasy-looking gray cat rubbed against my leg and I brushed it away. Nana said us two was making biscuits and gravy together, so find some flour in the cupboards. I rooted through the tin cans without labels and brown paper sacks full of nuts and dried peppers. Biscuits and gravy sure sounded good. Since Fever and Ma had three jobs each, usually, and spent their extra time out with their pals, I always got my own food—the cereal was in the box and the soup was in the can, you know?

A empty metal sound flew in the open windows, making the cat bolt, but not surprising Nana at all. Spade must've got the washer to where he wanted it. Nana leaned down near the front burner on the stove and held out a lit match. She was awful close, but her hair didn't catch fire.

—Wyatt! Where are you? GET OUT HERE! Uncle Spade hollered.

—SHUT UP OUT THERE! Nana hollered back, brushing a dirty curtain out of her way and leaning over the sink. HE'S ALREADY HELPING ME IN HERE. WE'RE MAKING SUPPER.

I leaned in behind her to see Uncle Spade by the shed holding three more of those plaster midgets.

—SUPPER? he called back. NO, BREAKFAST, MA. HE'S COOKING? COME ON.

—DON'T COME-ON ME. THE BOY IS HELPING ME COOK.

—OKAY, BUT—

—NOT OKAY. YOU SHUT YOUR MOUTH AND GET TO WORK. WE'LL CALL YOU WHEN BISCUITS IS READY.

Nana clattered a fry pan onto the lit burner. I really wanted to go outside and get away from the mildew smell, but it never seemed like there was much choice with Nana. I watched Spade take the elf-things around the shed to the ditch and heard them smash against the washer. Nana didn't pay attention. She just scooped some white butter out of a tin can with her fingers and dropped it in the pan, wiping the rest on the front of her housedress.

—Find that flour?

I placed the open bag carefully in her hands. She got to work, asking for a spoon or a slab of bacon from the fridge. Everything I found and handed to her, she held up to her face and checked

18

out. I wondered if her seeing was like looking up through the surface of the water in the tub. Or like after crying. I squinched my eyes up and looked through my eyelashes, all the lights and reflections stretching and smearing like wet paint. You don't really think about other people being different until you meet somebody like Nana.

As she put the biscuits in the oven, she asked me why we were visiting, and I bit the inside of my cheek. I stopped blurring my eyes. I wondered what I should tell her. Maybe she already knew and was testing me. . . .

—I don't know, Nana, I said. It's just a trip.

—Spade don't come visit but once a year and this is number two, so I figure he needs something. Instead he brings you— Did we make the coffee yet?

—No, Nana, it's in your hands.

—I don't understand him looking all over for something when there ain't nothing to find.

—Looking for something?

—Oh, he don't know what it is and I sure don't, but he's looking. Else he never would've left your papu and me, taking off with his big brother to the City. Didn't find it there neither, did he?

She shook her head as she closed the coffeepot and wiped her hands on her front again, then reached in a pocket and dug around. I didn't say nothing, just glad she didn't ask about my folks, 'cause I don't know if I could've told her the truth, and I sure don't think I could've explained my leaving. So I stirred the gravy, bits of bacon floating around in it, and waited. Finally she pulled out Papu's old tobacco pipe and slid it between her lips, the plastic tip clacking against her teeth. She didn't light it, just sucked on it. That was just one of her weirdo things, like holding them pieces of broke glass up to the light and looking through them one by one when she thought we weren't looking.

—I'm just afraid if he don't watch out, Franklin's gonna run right off the end of the earth.

I laughed.

—Why you laughing? If you don't take care, he might drive you off the edge with him.

—But Nana, there ain't no end of the earth. You mean, into the ocean?

She took the pipe out, clicked her tongue, and said:

—Oh, I see. You been educated in city schools. Sit down and let me tell you something. You're still young enough to unlearn the lies. See, the government tells you there's all kinds of things out there—space and Communists and Arabs—but we all know there's three places only, heaven and Earth and hell. Holy Bible says so, don't it?

—But Nana, there's lots of photos of space and news shows on TV about Arabs.

—You ever been to space? Nana leaned forward, shaking the chimney end of the pipe. YOU EVER KNOW A ARAB, A REAL TURBANED PERSON?

—No, I said, my voice tiny. But Nana . . .

—Wyatt, I am telling you not to trust pictures and not to trust the government. You got to trust in God. He provides.

I raised up out of my seat a little, stretching my neck to see if I could find my uncle, see if maybe he was coming inside soon. I thought she had to been joking with me. Possibly she was going to laugh in a minute, like Spade does sometimes, and slap me on the shoulder, saying something like, *I sure got you good*. But she just kept going, and I couldn't exactly argue with her, could I?

—Wyatt, tell me. You ever see a curve in the earth?

—I seen hills.

—Hills, sure, but a CURVE to the land? No? 'Cause there ain't none. The world's flat.

—But we don't got to see the curve to know it's there.

—You think like that and you'll fall into the pits of hell. Go ahead. Follow him in.

—Maybe we could travel and find the edge and just look over?

—Can't just look over into hell without your soul getting sucked straight down in. You see what I'm saying? Folks need to stay in one place. I live off this land. Never gone more than thirty miles from here, because there ain't no need.

—WHAT THE HECK ARE YOU TWO GIRLS DOING IN THERE? Spade hollered from the back porch, kicking dirt off his boots. Nana leaned in, fumbling to find my knee, and squeezed it tight with her nails.

—You think about it good and hard, Wyatt, she whispered. Your uncle, he won't listen.

—Yes, Nana. I'll think about it, I said, looking toward the screen door as he swung it open, carrying a red plastic box. Nana stood up and announced that the biscuits would be done as soon as we scrubbed our hands.

I went to the sink, avoiding both of them. I wanted to bust out the window screen, scramble out, and run to the woods. I was trying hard to get along with everybody and be good, but all they did was confuse me and get me peeved.

—You ain't too used to cooking, now, are you, kiddo? 'Cause after we eat, I'm taking you out back and putting you to work. Hard labor. Something you have to learn. Not this cooking crud. Got me?

—Franklin, Nana said, eyeing the box. Get that off my table.

—Come here, Wyatt. You got to see this. My old tackle box.

Uncle Spade opened it up to three different drawers full of feathers, threads, and wire. He pulled out one that sort of looked like a hooked wasp and handed it to me, telling me how he'd made all them lures with Fever when they was kids.

I nodded, saying nothing, still peeved at him and Nana and not caring what box of junk he'd found.

—GET IT OFF MY TABLE, Nana yelled, so he scooped up the box and dropped it by the upstairs steps.

We sat, and I watched Nana bow her head to pray for us. Then we ate, not talking, and I was happy for the quiet. Nobody in my family made any sense. Ma wore this gold cross on a chain but never went to church. Her and Fever and Spade all said their Jesuses and Christs like they was cusswords. And now, the first time anybody was talking God stuff, I was getting hollered at. Nothing was ever just said. It was either shouting or quiet. As I chewed, I got to thinking maybe I wasn't really related to a single one of them. Only problem was we all had the same pasty white skin, leaf green eyes, and scraggly black hair. But how could I feel so different on my insides? I didn't want to holler at anybody. I didn't want to be hateful. I just wanted people to be happy, maybe smile sometimes, you know? And I didn't want to be alone, like everybody else wanted to be. I was so scared of being left on my own, but right then, feeling so peeved and confused, I just kept staring at the kitchen window, picturing busting out, running as fast and as far as I could.

CHAPTER FIVE

I DIDN'T BUST OUT THE kitchen window, and that night Uncle Spade didn't leave me. Instead, when it was still dark out, he whipped my blankets off me and made me come fishing with him. Boy, was he excited. Kept talking at me the whole time, but I stayed quiet. My skin felt itchy, burning from not enough sleep, so I pretended to be happy. He'd already packed up the Chevy with a bunch of junk and given me this can of worms I had to hold the whole ride.

When we stopped, it was still dark out. Him and me lugged everything down near a stream—rods and food and beer and stuff. As the sun started coming up, even before bothering to open his coffee thermos, Uncle Spade showed me how to stab a worm on a hook.

—What you do is double the sucker up, triple him if he's a big one, he said, like this. See, I push it on near the top and let it dangle down in a loop. Wyatt, don't just stand there like an idiot. Grab one and do what I'm doing. . . . There you go, just grab it. DON'T DROP IT. . . . Yeah, there, and push it on, then loop it around so he still squirms and then push it through the other end of him like this. See? Okay, now you. NO, no, no. You're mangling him. LIKE THIS . . . Okay, now we're ready.

And he handed me a pole. But I really didn't want to fish. I don't even like fish sticks.

—No, no, no . . . not like that, he said. You got to tilt your arm and arch it, extend the rod out at your side. You look like a sissy. I bet you can't even toss a baseball. Be a man. Watch me do it. Just watch. See . . . Okay, now you try. . . . That's a little better. You really got to practice. You got to appreciate what you're doing here. . . . Oh, Jesus. That'll scare the fish away. Light and easy. Don't give me that look, just follow what I'm doing here. . . . Now let it set in the water like that till you get a bite or till it floats too far downstream. Got that?

And on and on and on he talked, me biting my lip and trying hard, but really waiting to be done. Problem was, I didn't want Uncle Spade to leave me at Nana's. So I had do whatever he told me, no matter how tired or grossed out I got. I watched the sun come up and show me where we were: Spade and Fever's favorite spot. It looked like we were the only two people who'd been there in a long time, 'cause there wasn't the empty bottles and condoms and potato chip wrappers that you normally find at the edge of a river. The water was real clear and cold. We finished the coffee. He finished a smoke. And we just stood there.

—I don't understand you, kiddo, Spade said, plopping the first fish into an old dented pail he'd filled with stream water. You're acting like this is work. I'm telling you, fishing ain't work. It's relaxation. It's sport. We don't got to fish for food.

I nodded and tried to smile. My uncle handed me a sandwich. We ate standing there, shifting from foot to foot, never setting the poles down, never sitting to take a break. He finished a beer. I finished a pop. He caught three fish and had to toss a tiny guy back before I got my only one.

—According to where the sun is, it's almost nine o'clock, he said.

I didn't know if that was true or not and I didn't care. I was more than ready to go. He handed me the pail of fish, the water sloshing on my leg when I walked. I was glad my fish wasn't the smallest so he couldn't rib me about it. It was second smallest. The biggest was the size of my foot.

—Bring that bucket over here, Spade said, standing by a little white hut near the trees, laughing at me.

I sloshed the bucket over, and when I got closer, I could see a old table and stool inside. The fish-cleaning shack. Fever and he'd built it with Papu. Grinning at me, Uncle Spade swung open the creaky screen door with no lock. I don't think I'd ever seen a door with no lock before. In the City, we always locked ourselves in *and* out of every place. The tiny shack stunk like old fish and rotted wood. If it hadn't had screen walls, I'd've smothered, I swear.

Man, I sighed real deep; I thought we were leaving, but we had to stay to clean the fish. Spade opened a drawer in the table to pull out a huge, wood-handled, horror-movie knife. I thought the fishing was the test for me, proving how I'd do anything for him, making him want to keep me around, but now his real test was happening. So I stayed quiet and spread newspaper on the table like he said. Laying out each sheet, I found the comics (Garfield sleeping in his tiny bed and Dagwood smiling up at me, happy in bright colors and joking around with their words in little clouds above their heads).

—Snap out of it, kiddo. Would you? Watch carefully, 'cause you're gonna fillet yours.

He yanked a fish out of the pail, slopping water over the sides, and slapped it down on the paper, pressing his palm over it, forcing it to stop squirming. One wet eye stuck to the paper and made the cartoon colors bleed. Slits in its head flapped open and closed, faster and faster. It was the grossest thing I'd ever seen. I don't think I'd ever been that close to a live animal before, except for one school trip to the City Zoo, but there they had bars and fences to keep us from touching. Jeez, that shed made me want to puke. *Please don't puke*, I told myself. *Show him you're tough.*

Spade started talking and moving super fast.

—Okay, kiddo, first grip the knife tight and chop off its head right behind the eyes like this—*CHUNK*—and then slide it out of your way. Now turn it so you can get to its belly, like this, and angle the blade along that line you can see between the scales. See it? Okay, now slit it all the way to the tail and open it up to get at the guts so you can scrape them out of the way. Chop the tail off if you want, but I like leaving it on. Once you're done with the insides, pick it up, flip it over, and—this is the tough part—you got to scale it by slanting the knife edge like so. Scrape it against the scales and they pop right off. See? Oh yeah. There we go.

And they did pop right off, shooting all over, covering Spade's hands. They looked like a baby's yanked-out finger-nails. It was sick. When he finished, he held up two clean pink-ish white slabs. He tossed them on a fresh piece of newspaper.

—Remember, you got to chop its head off quick, before it even feels the pain.

That *CHUNK* sound bounced around in my head, that fish eye staring at me from the pile of gunk. I didn't know it'd be so hard to watch. *CHUNK* and it was dead. That easy. My mouth got dry and tasted like old newspaper.

—You got it, Wyatt? Let me show you again. Watch carefully.

I stared through the scales to Dagwood chomping down on one of his gigantic sandwiches. That was funny, real funny. . . . *CHUNK* and the second one was dead. Spade's hands flew like they were doing all the thinking, not stopping or caring at all. That's why they call him Spade, that quick hand slicing through any animal, it didn't matter: gopher, rabbit, squirrel. *CHUNK* went their heads. Now I'd seen it with my own eyes.

—Wyatt, watch. Now the scales. Right? Scrape at a angle and . . . He kept talking at me, dangling the fillets in front of my nose, then tossed them over with the first two. Dunking his hands back in the water where scales floated, he pulled out his third fish, the biggest.

—The catch of the day, he said. The winner. Help me hold this baby down, will you?

The fish fought back hard and wouldn't stay still. Spade grabbed my hand and guided it to the tail end, which shoved up against my palm. The fish pushed and pushed to get away. The scales scraped at my skin and I shuddered. Spade grumbled.

—Come on, sissy.

Spade's shoulders hunched. He grabbed the knife and *CHUNK*, the winner stopped moving, his head swept to the pile by the blade.

—Would you look at those devils? Better than steak. THAT IS PERFECTION.

The word "perfection" echoed in the woods.

—Sure are big, I managed to choke out.

—Now, my boy, it's your turn to cut. Step up to the plate and get your catch.

He made room for me to see into the pail where the little guy circled frantically. It wasn't the fish I caught. He'd left me the littlest one. I looked up at my uncle.

—Well, what're you waiting for? Spade asked.

—That ain't my fish, I told him, pointing. He said it was mine and we argued, but I wanted him to know I caught only the second smallest. I wasn't the loser. I had to prove it, but I got all shaky, knowing I was just getting him peeved. Finally he told me to shut up and grab the dang thing. I touched the water and stopped. He was so tiny and scared. I didn't want to kill him, but I felt trapped. In the pail, the fish slipped from my grip.

—Stop fooling, Spade said, elbowing me aside and pulling it out. Here. Take it.

He slapped the little guy into my hand and I set him on the gooey comics, easing my hand down over him. I guess I just didn't push hard enough, 'cause he slipped away and tried to wriggle free, bending and arching across the table, his mouth gaping open, strangling on the air.

—Boy, get a hold on the freaking thing. YOU'RE MAKING IT SUFFER. Grab it. Chop the head off. QUICK.

The fish flopped into the corner against the screen, staring me in the face. I grabbed for him, but he started jumping around again. Spade yelled louder and louder until he finally swore with the worst cusswords ever, punched the door open, and stomped to the Chevy. He opened the trunk and pitched things in one by one, still yelling about what I was and what I was doing to the fish. He was leaving me there. I knew it and started shaking.

I placed my hand over the fish, pushed down hard, and just stared at Garfield's eyes. I laid the blade behind its gills. Looking quickly into his eye, I pushed the knife down as hard as I could and—*CHUNK*—cut through to the paper, tearing it and scratching along the wood. Dead. Spade stopped yelling. No noise anywhere. I bit my lip. Spade shut the trunk and stopped to watch me. I slid the head to the pile and finished cleaning it as best I could. The fillets were mangled to shreds, but I held them up for Spade to see.

—Okay. Wrap them up and let's go, he said from far away.

I cleaned up the papers and guts, then wiped the knife off and put it back in its drawer. I carried the pail and the wrapped fish back to the Chevy. Spade took our catch from me and set it on the seat next to him.

—Sit in front. We'll take these back to Nana. She makes a mean fry batter. That is, if she can see to make it. She might just fry up one of my shoes.

CHAPTER SIX

UNCLE SPADE LAUGHED

and talked all the way back to Nana's, blaring the radio, speed-ing, me sitting next to him, my feet up on the dashboard, not worried for a little bit.

But man, I really hated having to cut up them poor fish. I only killed stuff three times in my life, and that fish was the first. Second time was a couple years later, after I got used to Uncle Spade not leaving me and used to staying with him, used to moving around all the time and used to all his ladyfriends.

See, my uncle's got ladies across the whole country (and, he said, one named Inez in Mexico). They was like the freckles on my body—you could find one almost anywhere, even when you weren't looking you could be surprised. Some lived in the same towns, maybe working together at the mall. He had a list of standards that they had to meet. He told me, *never ever* let them know they meet the standards. Of course, that list changed a lot over the years. Especially once I started staying with him, 'cause I needed a place to sleep.

I stayed quiet and separate from Uncle Spade's ladies as best I could. If I got too attached, like with Lynnesha, then I'd just get hurt. I had to remember I was a visitor wherever we was.

—We're only staying long enough to rest and fill up, Spade'd always say.

We'd fill up on food or sunlight or TV. I filled up. Uncle Spade, he overfilled and then couldn't take it. He swelled up from their goodness and had to go, empty out, and fill up with somebody else. So I was polite as I could be and stayed out of the way and slept on the floor. And before I knew it, we'd step out onto a foggy morning driveway with our bags, revved by the excitement of newness when the Chevy stopped again.

I don't remember all of them, and there sure was a whole stack of one-timers, but the most important one, of course, was Lynnesha in Iowa. She was my favorite. Her voice reminded me of cream swirling into coffee. Olive, she worked the carnival circuit and liked to pretend she was made of money (thanks to her I got my first tie). In the summer, when we swung through Minnesota for the state fair, Nelly'd let us park the Chevy on her lawn for free. She'd wait on her roof for my uncle to bring her back stuffed animals and beer from the midway. And in the winter we'd stay in Irma's funny wood house hid by trees in Utah. Irma thought my uncle was a Bible salesman and taught me to ride a horse. And then there was Lane, a real Texas lady, like out of a black-and-white movie. We never stayed in her mansion behind the long white fence, 'cause her husband, she said, wouldn't let us.

Guys came from every corner of Tennessee to see Star dance on tabletops, but every time Uncle Spade showed up at the Roadside Rambler, she'd hop out of the spotlight and walk to the door he held open, hollering how she was leaving for good. Hubcap Sandy smelled like car grease and roses, and lived above her car garage in Washington (the state). We usually left her place running, Uncle Spade taking a black eye with him, and Sandy hurling car parts and empty whiskey bottles out her window.

—THAT WAS MEANT FOR YOUR BLEEPING UNCLE, WYATT, NOT YOU, she'd shout. I'd wave up at her, one sneaker dragging on the cement before I could pull it into the already moving Chevy. Then there was Edie, the little wacky artist who made my head itch; she was so hyper it seemed like she'd spin out her trailer door into the Arkansas fields. We couldn't never sneak off on her, 'cause Edie never slept. I swear. Out of all his ladies, she always had to know when we was heading off. Sometimes it was to sell her art at corner stores and gas stations.

We was staying with Edie when I made my only real friend.

I'd had school pals before, but nobody who liked me just 'cause. He sat alone at the Uncle Sam's Trailer Park Annual Cookout on a picnic bench, burning his name in a dry leaf with a magnifying glass. His too-big Amoco jacket and bug eyes behind beer-mug glasses looked funny, but I walked over anyway and said hi, smiling big as I could. I'd been standing around, so bored my eyes blurred, listening to the guys talk meat at the grill while the ladies sat in a circle of kitchen chairs, ignoring their crying babies. The sky lost the sun, so he looked up and said hi back.

—Clark? I asked, reading the black circle burns on the leaf.

He nodded his head. I told him I was Wyatt and staying with Edie, my uncle's ladyfriend, the one in the pink tank top over there mixing the fruit salad. Did he know her? He'd seen her around. I told him we just got in the day before. My traveling salesman uncle and me, his assistant.

Clark and me, we shook hands like guys do, his only as big as my palm. Then we took off, him and me, forgetting to eat, not telling nobody. He wanted to show me this place called Feegler's Quarry. As we ran, he told me all the stuff he had in his pockets: Bazooka bubble gum, a fistful of firecrackers, some plastic-wrapped toothpicks, a lighter, and his magnifying glass. I showed him my piece of Nana glass, my pocket knife, and ten dollars I kept for emergencies. Then he told me all the stuff we'd find down there past the NO TREPASSING sign at the bottom of a hole the size of a baseball field. He was right.

There was piles of trash scattered between big rocks: broke sunglasses, old ovens, dented tin cups, cracked mirrors, a dirty-crusty girl's barrette I clipped into Clark's hair and he tugged out, lonely shoes, a iron without a cord. We picked through it all till we got to the edge of a mossy pond.

—Those tadpoles are huge, Clark said, his words echoing just a little.

—Those what?

—Baby frogs, Wyatt.

The mud at our feet wriggled. He hunched down, hands on his knees, and I squatted just like him, told him to grab one, but he bunched up his nose under his big glasses.

—You, he said.

There must've been hundreds of them, all swarming. Clark explained that the water'd gone down from pond to puddle, so the almost-frogs had to fight for space. I swallowed, remembering my fish. I trapped a giganto breath in my chest and snatched up a plum-sized one, slick like wet plastic. Baby arms and legs poked out his sides but didn't work too good. Tail flapping was all he could do. I had to hold him just right to keep from crushing him into oozy pieces. Clark pulled my hand below his freckled nose, breathing on my arm.

—Give me your magnifying glass, I said, suddenly excited.

—Why?

His hands rattled around in his pockets full of junk.

—So I can see it better.

I did want to see the little guy better, but I also wanted to see what he'd do if I tried burning him like Clark burned the leaf. Gross, I know.

—You know, Clark said, wiping the magnifying glass off with his shirt, these are called polliwogs, too.

—You're a polliwog, I said, yanking the toy out of his hand.

Under the glass, the tadpole's skin looked like pond water, sparkling and deep. I moved the shadow of my head to aim the sun on the tadpole's back, then focused the circle of light smaller. Its skin tightened up and tore, turning black.

—Don't do that, Clark said, snatching back the magnifying glass.

—Why not?

I was braver now. I'd proved it. And Clark was scared, not looking up at me.

—Let's see if I can chuck it up to the top of the quarry.

—Why? Clark asked, tilting his polliwog head up at the ledge.

—Just 'cause, I said.

I didn't know why I was acting like that, like all of a sudden I was a totally different guy.

—Okay, Clark said real serious. Do it as hard as you can.

For a second I held the tadpole over my shoulder, slung back like a baseball pitcher. A train whistled in the distance. Then I threw it so hard my shoulder popped. We watched, our mouths open. It spun end-over-end into the sky, a dot on the clouds. I rubbed my shoulder. My heart pumped behind my ribs. The dot curved down, dropping quick, and splattered against the quarry wall. It left a wet spot on the stone before dropping into the shrubs. My stomach clenched. I checked Clark's face before saying anything. His mouth spread into a wide grin.

—COOL, he said. So I said:

—Yeah. Man oh man. Cool.

—Wyatt, do it again. Really smash one good. Huck it straight at the wall this time.

I reached back in the mud for a bigger one. Its tail was almost gone. And I killed that one too—threw it straight at the quarry wall. I didn't think about it. I just closed off my brain. We killed three more like they was nothing. Clark helped. He might not've smashed them on the far wall, 'cause his only made it into the scraggly shrubs, but he kept pushing me.

—Do it again, Wyatt. Do it again.

When he got bored watching, he dug the firecrackers out of his back pocket. Waving one under my nose, his eyes shining through his glasses, he told me:

—Here, stick this in its mouth and I'll light it.

—No way, I said, and I raised the tadpole above my head, out of his reach. He was the biggest one so far, with whole arms and legs.

—No, stick it in his butt, I said.

I felt crazy. Clark gripped my elbow, grinning up at me, and we laughed.

—No, just his mouth and I'll light it. Then you throw him straight up. Come on.

Laughing made it okay. The puckered mouth felt soft-hard like my ear. Clark quick jabbed the firecracker in and lit it before I could think. My heart burned hot, considering my hand might get blown off. The smoke smelled sour. The fuse sizzled. I threw him up. We darted in different directions, out of the way, ducking, but keeping our eyes on him.

As the big guy started falling, his arms and legs spinning, he popped, scattering wet chunks all around us. A red piece of guts hit my shoe. With the others the wall had been far away. This was a real animal, bloody inside, not like a fish.

—SICK! Clark hollered, dropping the other firecrackers and swiping globs from his hair.

I kicked the piece off my shoe, holding in a scream.

—HEY! YOU THERE! WHAT'RE YOU DOING?

A tall, pruney old man stood next to his truck by the NO TRESPASSING sign, shouting:

—CAN'T YOU READ? GET OFF MY LAND!

—It's old Feegler. Come on, Clark whispered. This way.

He took off, ducking like the old guy might shoot at us. I followed, weaving through the bushes to a cool damp crack between the rocks that led up to the woods. I looked back at old Mr. Feegler waving his orange hunter's cap, his mumbled shouts bouncing around his hole-in-the-ground as we reached the top. Covered in mud and cuts from thorny bushes, we ran back to the barbecue and fell on the ground next to each other. Everybody leaned over us, asking where we'd been, what we were running from, what we'd done now, and I felt the cleanest sweat I'd ever felt run off my skin and the sweetest air I'd ever breathed cool my lungs.

CHAPTER SEVEN

I GUESS IT LOOKED

pretty funny once us two started playing together, more like a
dad and a son than just two regular kids, one too big and the
other too small. But Clark was more like the dad the way he told
me things: *Wyatt,* he'd say, *see how the bees poke their tongues in
the daisies to drink and that yellow stuff sticks to their legs? They
pass it to another flower and that's pollenization, how the flowers
turn to seeds. Get it?* Stuff like that. Not the way Uncle Spade
made up junk to tell me, like: *See, kiddo, the black squirrels are
the boys and the gray ones are the girls.*

I'd ask Clark more questions than he could answer. But he'd
try explaining most of them, 'cause I was the first not to laugh
at his name. *Cool,* was all I said, and he smiled, 'cause most the
schoolkids teased him. See, Clark's name changed when his ma

got a new husband, Mr. Kent. So it wasn't like his folks planned on torturing him. That day with Clark I killed for the second time and decided I didn't want to do it ever again.

We ate them fish that Nana cooked. I choked down the small one and nodded my head to everything Spade said, while he ate *my* fish. When they weren't looking, I dropped bits to the huddle of cats till they started fighting over them and Nana got upset.

—GET THEM BEASTS OUTTA HERE! HOW'D THEY GET IN HERE, ANYWAY?

—Ma, they're your cats.

—No they ain't, she said, kicking at them with her brown slipper.

She wiped her mouth on her sleeve, and Spade forced a burp. I sloshed the lemonade around in my mouth to get the fish taste out, and after we ate, Uncle Spade and me did some work around her house. Nana found me a old pair of my dead papu's work boots, then Spade showed me how to use a lawn mower. I pushed it around while he chopped down "widow makers." That's what they call the dangly branches, ready to break off and kill a man. I liked being outside, not thinking too much. It felt like Clean Time, sliding by with nothing wrong in the world. While we was working, Nana disappeared, and neither of us noticed till a couple hours later. We was cleaning her floors when she come back in the front door, one of her brown slippers missing. The other was covered in red mud. Her housedress had a tear, and long scratches ran up her legs. I cracked my knuckles, not knowing what to do.

—Where'd you go, Ma?

—Out for a walk.

—Where's your slipper, Nana?

—Don't you sass me, boy. Franklin, you tell him to shut up.

—Ma . . . you're all cut up and muddy.

—I'll go to the bathroom now. Put these in their crates.

She held out three pieces of glass in her muddy palms. I could see crusty blood between her fingers when she handed them to me. Watching her climb the stairs, I got this funny lump in my throat.

—There ain't nothing we can do about her, kiddo, Spade said. Just put that glass in the crate, and make sure you get it with the right color or she'll have a fit.

—Why's she collect it?

—She likes looking through it. I don't know.

Spade stroked the edge of his mustache.

—But why's she look through it?

—Jeez, just finish sweeping, will you? Let her have her glass. . . .

During supper Nana fell asleep at the table, chin on her chest. Spade woke her, but she grumbled at him:

—Leave me alone . . . always such a burden, Franklin, such a worry.

Once he got her to bed, he shuffled to the porch with a couple beers. I did the dishes quietly, so he wouldn't tease me for doing girl work, and saw him through the window sitting on the green couch. He rubbed chunks of Nana's glass between his fingers, watching the sun go down through them. I went to bed without saying nothing. Laying on the stack of blankets in the attic, I could feel my muscles ache from all the work, but I liked it.

In the middle of the night, I sat straight up, panting like a dog. A noise. Downstairs. The living room. Maybe the hallway. A eerie jingle. The grandpa clock? Sounded like somebody being strangled. I was sleepy-confused. Was Nana winding the clock in the middle of the night? I wrapped myself in a blanket and tiptoed down. If it was a robber, I'd punch him in the face. At the foot of the steps, I peered around the corner into the blue dark. Uncle Spade shut the clock door and sipped a beer. Clock said three fifteen. He wore his coat. He grabbed a ceramic pig-shaped jar from over the fireplace and stuffed a twenty-dollar bill inside, then pulled down the wood box where Nana hid Papu's pipe, sticking another bill there. Spade looked up and jumped, angry, whispering:

—What the heck are you doing up? Scared the stuff out of me.

—What are you doing? I asked.

—Nothing . . . Listen, we're leaving. Go get your gear.

—Why?

—I said get your gear.

—But I want to say good-bye to Nana.

—She told me to tell you good-bye, but she's too tired to get up. Now go, Spade said, waving his hand at me. Hurry up. I'll meet you at the car.

I gathered my stuff from the attic, folded the blankets up neat, and snuck down to Nana's bedroom door. The light was on, but the door was shut, so I set the blankets there. On my way out, I did grab a piece of glass, figuring she wouldn't miss it, a green piece that looks all sanded down and rounded off. I still keep it in my pocket. See? And I look through it sometimes. Makes the world look different.

CHAPTER EIGHT

SO UNCLE SPADE AND
me hit the road. I picture this crazy squiggled line we made
across the country—Wisconsin to Arkansas to New Mexico
to the Dakotas east to Rhode Island back to Idaho then New
Jersey to Georgia and on like that, wherever my uncle's deals
took us. Like with this one guy—I think his name was Phil,
'cause, well, they're always named Phil—he asked my uncle to
cross into Florida with three crates of M8os, so we put two in
the trunk and one in the front seat and took off. The summer
heat made me worry they'd all blow. Along the way we picked
up four more boxes full of beef jerky and Chick-O-Sticks for
half the normal price and Uncle Spade wrapped them in plastic garbage bags and strapped them to the roof. We stopped at
every country store just off the highway, where Uncle Spade

guaranteed freshness, talking smooth as the ice cream I'd eat on the front stoop listening to him, knowing the fireworks had to get dropped off in two days. We made it, no problem, and earned enough to eat steaks and potatoes that night. The next day we was driving down a gravel road, dust flying in the windows, and I knew my uncle was in a pretty good mood, so I got my nerve up and asked:

—Uncle Spade, what are you?

—What am I? He laughed and shook his head. I'm my own private traveling enterprise is what I am.

He flicked an ash out the window and grinned with one side of his mouth.

—I mean, like, what do you sell?

—What do you need?

—No, really . . .

—Yeah, really, he said, laughing real hard, smoke puffing out his nose, saying again, REALLY. What do you NEED?!

He did come out of stores and houses carrying full boxes. Sometimes he'd take the full boxes into another store or house. And sometimes I'd see things sticking out the top, like mugs or clothes or papers. Sometimes he'd hand me something. He gave me enough new jeans and T-shirts I had to get a suitcase. He tossed me a XXL sweatshirt with a huge truck on it crushing a car that was going up in flames: MONSTER TRUCKS MEAN BUSINESS. He'd hand me candy, toy guns, board games, notebooks, pens, and a rope. None of it I asked for. It was like getting stuff for school, but I didn't have to beg. I filled the back window of the car till he told me to move it so he could see, then I started filling under the seats.

That whole time, we never talked about my folks or how long I'd be away. I think Uncle Spade couldn't figure out a way to bring up the situation without having to talk about how much my folks hated me. He probably figured I'd bring it up when I was ready. I know he sometimes snuck off and called them, but I wanted to pretend we'd always been on the road together. The Chevy was my house. All his ladyfriends was my mom.

CHAPTER NINE

WHEN WE STOPPED AT

Lynnesha's, we liked to pretend we was settling in. Least I did. Oh, man, I remember seeing her for the first time. I seen just one of her eyes and knew she was beautiful. It was maybe five a.m. when we pulled up. Spade'd rung the bell, and Lynnesha opened her front door with the chain still hooked. Cold air snuck through the crack, making her breath look like smoke. She shivered and whispered:

—Franklin?

She peered through the gap with one eye, looking to see who he was with and make sure we wasn't messed up. See, Lynnesha always worried about her pretty house on that dead-end street when Spade came calling. Who could blame her? You never knew who or what he might be bringing with him.

Before bringing me, Spade'd brought lots of his bristly burping buddies, who'd bust in with bottles of whiskey and stogies to ash on her clean carpet while they played cards and cussed. And one time Spade brought his pal Bad Back Jack, who lived on her couch for weeks, shaking and puking until finally she made Spade drag him out. But sometimes he brought huge bouquets of flowers bursting open like fireworks that he pressed through that crack in the chained door, their petals touching her face. Most times, though, she wouldn't open the door for him unless he was clean and grinning and alone.

So when Spade showed up with tall, scrawny me wrapped in a blanket, pale and hunched over, she got real nervous.

—NO. No. No, she said. Franklin, NO WAY.

He begged her, pushing his nose into the crack and saying how long a drive we'd had, but she told him how she needed her sleep and her sanity and was sick and tired of him bringing his friends by her house in the middle of the night.

—Oh, Christ, this ain't no friend. It's my nephew, Wyatt.

I smiled at her, big as I could.

—Your nephew?

—I told you about him lots of times, Uncle Spade said.

—He on drugs?

—He's just a tired kid.

I rubbed my face with fists full of blanket and looked into her glittery eye. By this time, I'd already stayed with three or four of my uncle's ladyfriends, so I was used to them being a little shocked I was around. I had to prove I was harmless and would stay out of their way.

—Is he wearing a cape? she asked.

—Just let us in already. I been driving all night, Uncle Spade said, then sighed and whispered in a almost sweet voice I'd never heard him use before: Please . . .

The door shut, then the chain rattled free. She flipped the hall light on, letting me get my first look at her: smooth brown skin, thin hands clutching her robe shut, makeup still on from work that night, and silver barrettes twisting her hair up like a puff of smoke. Beautiful. The word really meant something then. *Beautiful*, I thought. Gosh, she made me nervous. I kept smiling as I followed Uncle Spade past her, 'cause when I don't people get worried.

—Thank you for letting us in, I said.

Spade introduced us, pointing first at her, then at me. And as I went to put my hand out, the blanket slipped off me. I picked it up, my cheeks red from my clumsiness, and put my hand out again. Staring at her long eyelashes and thin eyebrows, I told her it was nice to meet her. She smiled and asked me to come inside and warm up, so I walked into her living room, but stayed by the wall.

She turned to Spade, laughing like a little bird, and said:

—He looks like a mop turned upside down—same wavy pile of hair as you. Oh, and those freckles . . . He's a looker.

—Hey, you got any booze, baby?

Spade sat on the arm of her couch and wrapped himself around her waist, squeezing, pulling her between his legs. She wriggled around to get a kiss. He slid his lips down her neck. Ma and Fever didn't never do that kind of junk. It made my face burn even redder, so I turned away and looked at this one cabinet with all these matching silver frames full of black people posed in fancy clothes. She told Spade to stop and pushed him off.

—Excuse me, sugar, she said, squeezing my arm.

I flinched. I wasn't used to being touched. But she was just reaching for the whiskey on a shelf under the black-and-white photos, and I was in the way. As she reached up, she looked me right in the eyes and told me I had the biggest, widest eyes she'd ever seen.

—They're the color of maple leaves. Not like your uncle's, dark as the devil.

—Thank you, I said. Um, do you have a restroom?

I was kind of funny that way when I was a kid, trying hard to be polite and friendly as possible. Her thin eyebrows raised up, but she pointed at a door by the kitchen, then grabbed the whiskey bottle in one hand and three of her good crystal glasses in the other.

I locked the door to the bathroom and listened. Lynnesha was all worried about me, asking what my problem was, she

said I looked like I had a problem. My uncle told her I didn't
got no problem, I was just thirteen years old and needed to get
away from home for a while. She called him a liar and got him
peeved till he had a drink in his hand. He said he didn't want to
fight, and besides I wouldn't hurt nobody unless he told me to,
and he chuckled at his own joke. She didn't think he was funny
and told him she'd be watching me close.

I ran the water cold and splashed my face, then unlocked
the door and ducked out. I worried I'd bump something, bust
it, and make them mad, so I stayed still by the bathroom. That
place looked as good as any houses on TV, I swear. The white
walls was covered with dried flowers and more photos. Green
plants hung off her windowsills, and lamps made little islands
of light around the room. Lynnesha sat next to my uncle on her
couch, both feet on his leg.

—Come on in here and sit down, kiddo, Uncle Spade said,
waving his whiskey at me.

He told Lynnesha to pour me a whiskey too, but she looked
at me funny, then asked did I want milk. He told her I could
have a drink and told me I should and was pushing real hard till
I said I'd like milk, please.

—Wyatt, are you hungry? she asked, picking up the empty
glass.

I nodded and kept looking around, down the dark hall, out
the windows.

—What's wrong? she asked, slipping past me to the kitchen.

—Uh . . . well, where are we? I asked, leaning around the corner.

—Where are you? This is my house.

—Sorry, I mean, like where are we, what city?

—Franklin, you didn't even tell the kid where you were going? she asked, pulling out a milk carton and some cheese from the fridge.

—Jesus, he don't need to know. We're here. Wherever we are is here.

She watched me over the fridge door, probably thinking I was retarded.

—Here's your milk, sweetie. Hope cheese and crackers is okay.

—Thank you, Lynnesha, I said, and took the fancy glass and plate.

—You're welcome.

—This is a nice place, I blurted.

—Well, make yourself at home.

—Thanks, I said, gulping, feeling a little weird.

I'd lived in one place my whole life, but now I was moving all the time, and that night, suddenly, I woke up in the Chevy confused. I pictured a giganto map of the U.S. in my head and it made me feel like I was floating in a boat on endless water.

Lynnesha tilted her head way back to look me in the eyes. With one more gulp, I finished my milk and said:

—I. Feel. Lost . . . My uncle, he travels all over all the time and he don't care where he is. He just makes himself at home wherever. . . .

—He sure does.

She looked at Spade slumped over, his head on his own shoulder, asleep. For a minute she stood next to me, watching Spade, neither of us knowing what to say. By then the sun was like butter melting through the curtains. I could hear chickadees waking up. The whiskey started to slip from Spade's grip.

—I think I better get your uncle to bed.

—I'll carry him, I told her.

She slipped the glass from his hand. He made some grumbling noises as I slid my hands under him. I carried him easy as a bag of groceries to Lynnesha's bedroom, where the curtains kept the light like night, and set him on the bed real slow. She told me she'd get me some sheets and a pillow for the couch, but I explained how I was too big and the floor was better for me, really, it was okay. She didn't like that too much but pulled a pillow and blanket from her closet. For a minute Lynnesha just looked at me, my head almost bumping against the light hanging from the ceiling. I made no sense to her, I guess.

—Are you really thirteen?

—Yeah, just thirteen now, I said, and followed her to the living room.

—I haven't been around a lot of children before, she said, and looked me straight in the eyes. Wyatt? You're a good boy, aren't you?

—Yes, I am, I said, hugging the pillow.

She turned, saying good night, and headed to her room. I lay down and looked at the sun coming in through my piece of Nana glass till I fell asleep.

CHAPTER TEN

THE DREAM'S ALWAYS

the same, but the place changes: The floor where I'm lying to sleep ripples and melts, and I see myself at Ma and Fever's, in their old dark living room. The mossy brown rug gets wet and I sink through it into lukewarm water. *Oh, no,* I think, *I can't swim. I'll drown.* But somehow I stir my legs and arms around to keep my head up. Muffled short breaths stab my chest. Soggy chips and empty soda-pop cans spread away from me, past Ma's couch and Fever's chair and the TV that throws fuzzy blue light across the water. I paddle like a dog, trying to get to the linoleum in the kitchen or the hall, but Ma's couch bobs in my way. I try scrambling up the back, but my weight shoves it under. The cushions fill with water and drop into the dark with a cloud of mini-bubbles that tickle my skin. I swipe bobbing plastic army men out of my way. The kitchen floor is water. The hallway, too. I can't go nowhere. Then something below brushes my ankles. As I kick at it, my head ducks and my mouth fills with water that tastes like bad lettuce and cigarettes. I cough it out, drifting into the middle of the room. The microwave creeps into the doorway, surrounded by wood spoons. Then comes the noise. A tiny splash far away. Another splash down the hall. More splashes move closer and echo. This puny fish with copper scales flashes out of the water. My skin pricks cold. Another fish leaps up high, showing Swiss Army–knife teeth that tear through the microwave like vanilla ice cream, sparks popping. A bunch more little fish jump out of the water, their teeth wrecking more furniture. I can't hear my breath no more. Just gnawing and flapping. They swim toward me, and I lean back. The ceiling's cracked. A big fish scrapes its cold-metal scales against my leg, but this time I don't move away. The first to bite goes through my stomach and out my back. The hole burns hot, but the hollow makes me lighter. I float with my eyes open, not flinching, a storm cloud of my blood covering the water. There are so many fish I can only see their shiny scales sparkle in blue TV light. First my left knee separates from me. Each of my toes separates like wine corks on the water. My backbone unzips. The swarm cleans me down to my eyeballs, watching my bones float away—no skin or brains or muscles. My eyes separate, one seeing the cracked ceiling, the other seeing down to where the fish disappear, their tails flashing silver into the black.

CHAPTER ELEVEN

I WOKE UP SCARED, MY
skin soaking wet, breathing real heavy. Sunlight flickered off
silver picture frames into my eyes. I felt my whole body heavy
on a hardwood floor. My brain throbbed. I kept my eyes closed,
tried to calm down, and listened (this was usually how I figured
out where I was each morning). I heard: A metal pan on a stove
top, my uncle's morning cough, the clack of a cup on a table,
footsteps, a screen door opening, and my uncle spitting.

I'd never felt so bad. Fish. Eating my body, I remembered.
That dark water still hung in my head. Where were the fish
from? Why the water? The fish were on TV. It was a show I
seen. Piranhas. National Giraffic Special and me alone. I was
maybe nine, curled up in the dark at Fever and Ma's house. I
remembered the fishes' jagged teeth and how they could take

a whole cow apart in seconds. Lynnesha's was the first time I had that nightmare.

—Don't spit in my yard, Franklin, Lynnesha whispered.

—Where you want me to spit?

—Swallow it.

An egg cracked and sizzled.

—It's after noon. You want to wake your nephew?

—YOU wanna wake my nephew?

—I'm awake, I said, stumbling to the kitchen.

—Good. Now I can watch the tube, Spade grumbled as he polished off a beer.

Lynnesha pulled a plate from the oven and handed it to me. I sat in a red plastic and metal kitchen chair and ate the fried eggs, wiping up the yellow with toast and gulping coffee between bites. All the little sounds—even chewing with my mouth closed—seemed bigger in the quiet. Even the wind in the grass reached into the room. Squirrels skipped across her roof. I wanted to think up questions to ask to fill the quiet, shake the piranhas out, but nothing came to me. Uncle Spade dropped his napkin on his empty plate and walked out, flipping on the TV. Football cheers bounced off the walls.

It wasn't real big, the house. The kitchen could've fit five or six people squeezed tight, and I took up most of the living room floor. That left the bathroom, hallway, and her bedroom, with a bed filling it mostly.

—You want more? Lynnesha asked, a wood spatula in her hand.

—Do you got more eggs? I asked, smiling.

—You want more? she said again, looking me in the eyes, not smiling back. I nodded and she flipped one onto my plate.

She scrubbed dishes and wiped the counter while I swallowed the last bite of white. I started to stand up but sat back down. Where was I going? I didn't want to bother my uncle or make a fool of myself pretending to know something about football.

—You need any help? I asked.

She smiled and asked:

—Would you take the garbage out?

Her smile made the piranhas go away.

—Can's behind the garage.

I set my plate and cup in the sink. She handed me two white bags, stuffed and twisty-tied. Her yard was a real one, with green grass and a tall tree and a wood fence. My bare feet liked the grass and cold ground under it. As I shoved the bags into the trash can, one busted open, spilling out a couple empty whiskey bottles, a broke hairbrush, some moldy flowers, and a gift card with hearts covered in coffee grounds and mushy fruit. I couldn't read the blurry writing on the card, but heading back to the house, I wondered who gave Lynnesha those flowers, knowing for sure it wasn't my uncle.

From the screen door, I watched Spade at the kitchen phone on the wall. He was saying something about swinging through town, and by the tone of his voice, I couldn't help feeling like maybe he was talking to Fever. Spade saw me looking in and pushed down the hang-up button with one finger, then hollered into the living room:

—I'll pay you back later, baby. It's just a couple of calls.

—No, you won't, she said back as she appeared in the doorway. You never pay me for anything. Not the food. Not the phone calls. Nothing.

—I'll pay you back right now. I got it in the car.

—Yeah, sure. Where you driving off to now?

—I'm getting the money!

He stormed out. Lynnesha watched him, fists on her hips—not moving, not even when the screen door slammed. He slammed the door again and stomped back in, slapping a wad of cash on the kitchen table.

—Here, he said, catching sight of me. Half grinning, he said back at her: Here's for the good time last night.

She grabbed the stack of cash and jammed it in one pocket of her jeans, the tail ends of the bills peeking out. Spade looked at me peering in.

—Come on, Wyatt, we're going.

I stepped inside, making sure the screen door didn't slam.

—GOOD, she shouted. Go far away.

—Woman's driving me to drink.

—Drink's driving you, she said, dumping the rest of his beer down the sink.

—Boy, you sure work hard to keep me around, Spade shouted, and slammed his fist on the wall on his way out. Before I could follow, he gunned the car engine and sped off. And there I stood with the doorknob still in my hand. Lynnesha turned off her TV and turned on the radio, soft piano sounds replacing the football noise. She poured herself the last of the coffee, then sat down heavy.

—Sorry, I finally said. I should have gone with him.

—Spade's a dog, she said into her coffee cup. He's a dang traveling salesman of God-knows-what. He's a drifter, a carouser with all the wrong friends, and always in the wrong place at the wrong time. HE MAKES ME SO MAD. Why? Why do I do this to myself?

I sat down, and she just kept telling me all about the pals Spade'd bring with him and what they'd do, like about Bad Back Jack and his month on her couch. She talked like I knew everything she knew, like adults do, and that's the way she'd always talk to me after that. She was real peeved and talked into her coffee so she wouldn't have to see who she was talking to.

—. . . and he never tells me anything. Not why he has a knife cut across his chest or stitches in his wrist.

—He got in a knife fight? I asked.

—He vanishes and appears without any warning, waving a stack of clean green bills or begging for a couple to tide him over till the next time. Or he's bringing people into my house who won't leave. Why's he do that? She stopped and looked at me. Sorry, honey. Not you. I mean, I can't keep living like this.

—Is he gone? I asked.

—He'll be back, she said. Probably just went to get drunk. Besides, now he's got you to care for. If there's one thing I know, it's that whatever happens, good or bad, I always get him back. . . .

—You need help with anything? I can—I mean, you tell me what to do and—

—No, she said with a sigh in her voice. She patted my leg. But you should probably go wash that trash off of you, honey.

CHAPTER TWELVE

AFTER SHOWERING, I

watched TV, letting the room get dark, until Lynnesha flipped on a light and told me she had to go to work. She had on a tight white shirt with a bow tie and black pants. Her eyebrows bunched up. She was thinking about whether she could leave me alone or not.

—I won't touch nothing while you're gone. I'll go to bed real soon.

—Your uncle won't be long, I'm sure.

—I'll be good.

—Let me leave you the number, and you call if you need anything. Okay?

—Okay.

—You've got your blanket and pillows there. Food in the fridge. Don't turn on the stove.

I nodded. I wanted something from her, but I didn't know what. I wanted her to pat my leg again or smile before she left, so I sat up straight and nodded, promising again that I'd be good.

I didn't have no nightmare later, just lots of little dreams like TV commercials flashing past fast—Fever and Ma's faces over and over. Fever pounding on the police car and Ma yanking out her hair. Uncle Spade came back when I was sleeping maybe. Or maybe in the morning before I woke up. He was at the kitchen table with frozen butcher-wrapped meat against his forehead when I got up. Underneath his eyes was black and heavy. All the lines on his face were sharper, longer. He mumbled to me and I nodded my head. I took a apple out the back door and sat on the steps in the sun. I would've made toast, but it would've popped up and made noise. Plus I'd promised Lynnesha I wouldn't use nothing in the kitchen.

I could still feel the dreams flashing in my head while I stared at the back tree with leaves shaped like open mouths, the branches fanning up to the sky. A squirrel, jumping across the grass, found a piece of junk to chew on. I hucked my apple core at him and missed.

—WYATT! my uncle hollered.

I hopped up and ran inside.

—I got some places to go, he told me. Got to see some folks. Come on.

—Where's Lynnesha?

—Out. Don't worry, kiddo. We'll come back tonight.

I got dressed and we left, driving downtown. It was lots smaller than the downtown at home. None of the buildings were taller than four or five stories, but lots was happening, and I watched it all. First thing we did was go to a shoe store, and to remind me how (even with his yelling) he could be the best uncle, Spade waved his arms and said real loud:

—Find my nephew the fanciest pair of sneakers you got.

He had these people running to the back room over and over.

—What do you mean, you don't have them in HIS size? Find them.

And I walked out of there with four pairs plus some flip-flops, all different kinds I didn't even need. I OWNED stuff I didn't even NEED! Do you know how that feels? He got me some Superman comic books, too, when we stopped at the drugstore for his smokes. It was all too much.

We spent the next few days getting up late, getting Spade's hangover gone, and driving off. I'd stay wherever he told me: on a street corner or a park bench or in the back of the Chevy. I'd sit quiet (not talking to no strangers) and watch things, like a lady with her wig slipping off and a little girl pushing a cat in a baby carriage. Downtown, I saw a police guy ride a horse in the street.

—You done good today, kiddo, he'd say at the end of each

day, like I'd helped him carry or sell. But all I did was wait. I didn't care. I got anything I wanted and nobody bugged me and I could read and draw and play and I stayed out of his way. He liked our deal. I bet he thought, *It's not so bad taking care of a kid. Anybody can do this.*

We didn't see Lynnesha much. We'd all eat a late breakfast together before my uncle and me left. Usually that was the only time we saw her. Later, him and me ate lunch on our own. We'd have a hot dog or a slice of pizza when we got hungry. At night, her and Spade met in the bedroom before she left for work, closing the door, letting me watch TV till I fell asleep.

The last day we were in town, Spade brought me some post-cards from a stack he had and tossed them in the car window, saying:

—Write home, why don't you.

He was just joking, but I looked at the pictures of puppies in hats and a barn in fuzzy light, wondering, should I? Could I write home? I put "Fever and Ma" on the address side of the puppy card with the month, 'cause I didn't know the day, and wrote:

> Hi. I am with Uncle Spade. We are doing good.
> He got me lots of stuff. He has a nice friend.
> She is black. I ate ice cream all day yesterday.
> How are you?

Then I stopped. I couldn't send the card. I didn't know where they was. And my throat got sore like when you're getting a cold. I made myself cough, then I opened the car door and spit like Spade. When he came back, carrying some buckets of chicken and a case of beers, he said:

—Okay, kiddo, we're having some fun tonight.

Before we go, he meant. Before we disappear, but he didn't say that. And as we headed for Lynnesha's to party, chicken grease hot in my nose, I cracked the back window and let the air take the postcard away, tumbling through the exhaust and onto some street I didn't know.

That night a bunch of folks came over, their parked cars filling her dead-end street. Lynnesha didn't have to work, so we stayed up all night, people coming in and stumbling out, shaking my hand, rubbing my head, and shouting. I drank ginger ale from a martini glass and kept one of Spade's smokes behind my ear, telling people I was drinking fancy whiskey, telling them I was twenty-four. I smiled at every one of them, saying I was Spade's little brother or his cousin from New York City or his business partner. Everybody laughed and patted my back—ladies with big red lips, guys with big beards, all kinds of folks. Even a lady with a bald head and a man tattooed everywhere but his face. Lynnesha swiped the smoke from behind my ear. Spade tried to fill my glass with rum. All the blurry-eyed old people stared at me from across the room and looked away quick when I caught them. It was the best party ever, you know, 'cause it was my first. . . . I wonder why people don't have parties like that every night?

We were gone by dawn. A clump of folks snored on the couch. Spade kissed Lynnesha's sleeping head while I took our bags out to the car. I'd got used to her place and thought maybe we could stay. I didn't get that we were just taking a break. We would really never stop moving till the very end.

CHAPTER THIRTEEN

A BIG GREEN BANNER
by the petting zoo for baby kids hung over a card table where
this old lady sat all crunched up like a turtle, smiling at all us
passing kids, no teeth in her mouth. The sign said:

CABE COUNTY FAIR PIG-CATCHING C*O*N*T*E*S*T
FUN FOR ALL KIDS 14 & UNDER, 5 P.M. SATURDAY, $2 ENTRY FEE,
$50 PRIZE, PROCEEDS BENEFIT THE DARCY PALIN WHEELCHAIR FUND.

—Sign up? she squeaked to a girl who wrinkled her nose and
kept walking.

I gripped the damp dollars in my pocket that Uncle Spade
had gave me to keep me busy while he did some business.
Fifty bucks'd buy lots of stuff, I thought. I wouldn't have to

beg him for fair money for a while, and I could buy six hot fudge sundaes if I felt like it. I'd never had my own real money before. And all I had to do was wrap my arms around some dumb animal and hold him down. I could do that. I slapped at a stinging on my neck, knocking a big hairy black fly to the ground between my feet. It'd bit me. My neck kept burning, and I stomped on the big bug wiggling its legs up at me. No more thinking—I was signing up.

—Sign up? the turtle lady peeped, stretching back her wrinkled neck so far I could see in her nose. Oh, goodness, sorry. You're too old.

—I'm just big for my age, I explained, smiling really big.

—Nope, nope, she said, one hand guarding a box full of money and the other tapping at a clipboard. Fourteen and under for the sign-up.

—I'm just fourteen, I swear.

She rubbed her hairy chin, then slid the clipboard toward me, grunting:

—Two dollars. Cash.

As I signed on line number seven and dropped two bucks into her open claw, she grumbled about how I looked too big, how I'd ruin it for the other children.

—Be back by five, she muttered, snatching her clipboard from me.

Uncle Spade and me, we'd finished nearly all the fair circuit for that summer. Business was good. At each one, Uncle Spade chatted up the carnies and booth vendors. Then my uncle'd go back to the car for more junk to sell or trade. At each fair I'd take the ten bucks he'd wave in my face and run off, kicking up horse-smelling dust and trying to figure how to make the money last longest.

I always spent a super-long time waiting. This time, after signing up for the contest, I rode the Russian Mountain roller coaster first, and then the Ferris wheel to look over the whole fair into fields full of black-and-white cows, and then I went into the Tunnel of Horrors but didn't get scared, not even when this ketchup-covered guy snatched at my arm. And after that, and eating a funnel cake, my money was gone, so I picked dandelions and rubbed the yellow on my knees like Clark taught me. I liked butter a lot. Then I chased a orange cat between the vendors' tents to see his bit-off ear.

—UNCLE SPADE! I shouted, letting the cat get away. He was sharing a loud laugh with a sweaty man and his watermelon belly. UNCLE SPADE, I SIGNED UP!

My uncle shut his mouth and dropped his stubby cigarette on the ground. I was bugging him, but I was too excited to shut up. I wanted him to be excited too.

—WHAT?

—I signed up. I'm gonna win fifty bucks just by holding on to a dumb old pig.

Both of them stared. I didn't want to talk no more, but I'd already started. Talking's tricky that way.

—Sorry about this, Phil, he said to Watermelon Belly.

—It's a contest, and you got to come see me win, okay?

—Listen, kiddo, you know not to butt in. We got a deal. . . .

—I swear, I just ran into you on accident chasing a cat and— and I wanted to tell you—

He grabbed my shoulder hard, his jaw muscles poking out under his ears.

—Yeah. Okay. Why don't you come back in a hour.

I nodded and pulled out of his reach. His smile spread wrinkles into his forehead as he turned to the Watermelon. For a second I stared at the back of Uncle Spade's T-shirt with the letters M-A-U-I wrapped in a fuzzy sunset, wondering what the word meant.

I didn't go back in a hour. I was extra peeved at him. Besides, my skin still hurt where he'd grabbed me. Instead I waited under a tree close to the contest. I swatted lots of flies and planned how to catch the pig—maybe yank his hammy little legs right out from under him or buy a rope and do like cowboys do. I was building cities from dirt but destroyed them when people started gathering around a fenced-in area.

Inside the ring, there was this hairy guy in yellow rubber boots spraying water on the dirt to get it mushy. Everybody watching leaned on the white fence, but I watched from under the tree, listening to them mumbling how big the hog would be and would it bite the kids and could the kids hurt the animal. I stretched my neck up like the turtle lady, trying to see the pig, 'cause I'd never seen a real live one before. I didn't know if I'd get kicked or bit either.

—But this was for kids, somebody at the fence said, it couldn't be a mean swine.

I killed a black fly biting my arm and tossed it into my dirt city. Man, those bugs were getting me ticked off. The teddy-bear guy opened a gate in the fence, then Turtle Lady started checking names off her list. I stood up and stretched, stomped on my city, and headed down the hill. As I walked through the gate, Teddy Bear looked up at me and shook his head. Most of the other kids didn't make it past my belly button. I didn't care—just 'cause I was tall didn't mean I wasn't a kid still. They spread out across the pen, screaming and giggling, nervous to get started. Me, I stood right in the middle.

Teddy Bear heaved the snorting, wiggling pig out of a crate, grabbing two of its feet and flipping it over, then scooped handfuls of mud up and smeared it on its fat belly. Three judge guys with big beards sat in fold-up chairs on a stage, looking from kid to kid and talking. The adults outside the white fence pointed out their kids to each other. Then Turtle Lady stepped up to a microphone in front of the judges, tilting her tiny head way back, and explained the rules—basically, catch the animal and keep it still for a ten-count and the money'd be mine.

—EVERYBODY READY? she shouted. All right, then. Good luck, kiddies. Have fun. On your marks . . . get set . . . GO!

Teddy Bear let go of the pig's legs and it hopped up, running. Half the kids darted toward the muddy pig, but the others darted out of its way, toward their folks, crying and reaching up to be yanked out, so half the competition was gone. Their moms and dads grabbed them and pulled them to safety, saying:

—It's all right. It's okay. Don't be afraid.

It got me laughing at what scaredy-cats they were. Then one fat girl dove in, her long brown hair flapping behind her. She got soaked as the bug-eyed pig slipped out from under her. Cheers started then:

—GO, CASEY!

—GET HIM, HERBIE!

—JUMP IN, PETEY!

I stood there with fists so tight my arms shook, just watching and listening, smelling the wet ground and the arcade grease. Two drunk guys in red prize wigs from the shooting gallery hollered:

—GRAB HIS TAIL!

The pig squealed high and long as a tiny blond kid in jean shorts slid his arms around its belly and held on tight, getting dragged a couple feet closer to me before he fell off, spitting mud out of his mouth. Then that fat girl scrambled up again and started shoving other kids out of her way.

—I'M GONNA GET YOU, she hollered, and swiped its back legs out from under it.

I thought maybe I should climb out like the scared kids, since the whole thing was so stupid. Besides, that poor pig was freaking out. I didn't need to wreck my overalls and wait around wet and cold just to get hollered at by my uncle.

But before I could decide, I got knocked over. The animal had shoved its head between my legs to hide, dragging its back feet with that fat girl still attached. My butt got soaked and people laughed—no, howled—and pointed at me, shouting:

—GOOD ONE, KID!

—WATCH OUT FOR THAT WILD BEAST!

—DON'T BOTHER GETTING UP!

Man, that got me peeved. See, that's one thing I can't stand: Nobody laughs at me. And the cold mud was sending shivers up my back. Fat Girl still hadn't let go and the two were in the corner wrestling. Her ma stood on the fence above her, hollering down:

—HOLD HIM, CASEY, PIN HIM. DON'T LET GO! DON'T, DON'T, DON'T!

But the pig slipped free and galloped toward a bunch of bug-eyed kids. Casey's ma still hollered down until the fat girl staggered to her feet, mud dripping in her eyes. Then, over her ma's hollers, came another:

—WHAT'RE YOU DOING, WYATT? YOU LOOK LIKE A FOOL! GET UP AND GO, KIDDO!

By the time I got up and swung around, my uncle was already turning away, laughing with the red-wigs who'd shared their pitcher of beer with him. I wiped my goopy hands on my hips. I'd get that darned pig. I'd kill it with my bare hands, and then Spade'd stop laughing at me. He couldn't do that in front of people. I wouldn't let him.

The hog squealed again. After a skid in the mud, Fat Girl Casey tumbled over the pig, which twisted out from under her and headed for its crate, blocked now by a band of kids. The blond kid was at it again, leaping into the air, but the pig swerved, suddenly facing me and not able to slow down. I breathed real slow, its brown-covered pink skin filling my sight. It was all I saw, its panting all I heard. I stepped closer, moving slow. I hated that rotten noisy animal, too scared to fight back or bite or just stop running, and my fist pulled back near my shoulder, then swung out and smacked against his flat ugly nose. The pig tumbled, pointy feet over head, then down onto its back.

The whole crowd gasped. Turtle Lady's microphone gulp showered everybody. The judges covered their mouths. I fell on the lardo hog, even though it wasn't moving, holding its body down like they told us to. I figured it was dead. I'd killed another poor animal and this time with my fist. The blond kid started bawling. People covered their eyes and shook their heads. The red-wigs hooted.

—YEAH, MAN, my uncle hollered into the quiet, and leaned over the fence.

Panting, I told him:

—See, Spade, I ain't no fool kid.

—Winner? No . . . , Turtle-Lady said, and covered the microphone, staring at the judges.

The red-wigs clapped and cheered for me. A few other people copied them, not sure what to do. None of the judges were smiling. One shook his head, another rubbed his beard, but the third one nodded. It got quiet as Turtle Lady uncovered the microphone and said:

—We . . . have . . . a winner. . . .

—THIS IS A JOKE, hollered Casey's ma.

Other parents grumbled about how I was too big, too mean, no fair punching, this was supposed to be fun, not competition. I rolled off the muddy lump as Teddy Bear stomped toward me and scooped up the body. I got up and followed him. As he set it back in the pen, the pig wiggled and squealed, weak and confused, but alive. I smiled. Everybody clapped loud for the pig. Uncle Spade hopped the fence and held my arm in the air as the blond kid's parents took him away. I climbed up on the platform with the judges, who shook my muddy hand.

—Our winner is . . . fourteen-year-old Wyatt Reaves from . . . where are you from? Turtle Lady asked.

—Clydesdale, my uncle said, lying into her microphone.

—Don't worry, everyone, the pig is fine, she said, handing me the cash.

She walked away, and none of the other kids said nothing to me. Casey screamed and kicked her ma. A little one cried in his dad's arms. But I didn't care. I won. And my uncle smiled at me, which he never does, and told me I'd done good, and nobody ever said nothing like that to me before.

As we drove away, their fireworks show shot off above the Chevy. My uncle took me out for steaks and let me have two desserts and chocolate milk, and he didn't even make me spend none of my winnings. All we did was talk like crazy and toast my fight with lots of drinks.

—You REALLY got a fist on you, kiddo. I had no idea. You know what you could do . . . , he said, real drawn out and staring across the steakhouse at our future in a mansion with horses and a swimming pool. . . . Now, I'm just thinking out loud here, but with a fist like that and some training, some working out, and some negotiations by your uncle Spade, you could be a REAL fighter. Don't say nothing. Just think about it. You got that kind of focus in you? Maybe we'd just try it out, train you a little and see if you like it. . . .

CHAPTER FOURTEEN

I NEVER SAID YES, BUT

I never said no, so I guess that punch pretty much changed everything.

Uncle Spade, he finished out the county circuit, but between fairs he started rearranging his business. At first it felt weird: him talking to me like I was one of his buddies, 'cause he was trying to be like my coach, sort of. He started making up training, having me make beer runs or help truckers stack grain bags in flatbeds or farmers pitch hay. Seeing a farmer taking on day workers, Uncle Spade'd pull to the side of the road, lean one elbow out his window, and call:

—You need a big guy who can work for cheap and twice as fast as these sons of whatever? Then to me he'd say, Get out the car, Wyatt, and show him.

So I'd unfold from the backseat and stand up, a head taller than any of the guys hoping for a job. Then my uncle'd leave me there for the day. But before he drove away, he'd remind me:

—This is a good workout for your muscles, kiddo. Best exercise around to get you ready for your first big fight. So focus, okay? And remember, you're eighteen, right?

That was the one rule: I couldn't be a kid no more. I was only fourteen, but if anybody asked, I just looked young. I worked whole days with other guys baking in the sun or freezing in the snow, while Uncle Spade, he'd go off and take care of business, returning for me at sunset. I didn't complain about the sore muscles or the blisters, 'cause I felt like we was working as a team, you know?

—You got to get in shape, my uncle explained. Every different kind of work helps a different way. Like detasseling (that's taking the tops off corn plants), well, that'll help you with quickness. You got to focus and work fast with your hands and eyes. And the lifting, like with grain bags, well, that helps you build up your shoulders and legs. See?

The beer run was one training I did wherever we were, at whatever time of day or night, in whatever weather. My uncle'd tell me he needed beer and I needed a jog. It went like this: First, we'd swing into some motel. Second, he'd get a room key and directions to the closest liquor store. Third, he'd hand over some cash and I'd change my clothes, feeling grumpy but knowing I had to go.

I tried to remember the directions as best I could and run as fast as possible. Lots of times I got lost. And lots of times I ran in the grass in some highway ditch, breathing in car fumes, just to find out no matter how much I begged or pretended to be old enough or showed Spade's ID, they wouldn't sell me the case. So I'd run back to tell him he'd have to drive over if he wanted to drink. Most times, though, there'd be no problem. I'd make the run, buy a case, and lug it back. I never once cheated, always running, no matter what. Sure, sometimes I slowed down to count telephone poles or to watch a bunch of birds fly in a V or 'cause rain got in my eyes or dust whirled around me, biting into my skin, but I always did my training.

My body changed after so much working out: lots of sore muscles, cuts, bruises, pulls, sprains, and breaks. You could see which muscle was laying just under my thin skin. My shoulders widened. Veins and freckles coated me. I stared at them in the mirror, surprised they were me. I tore out jeans like The Incredible Hulk. I could crack a broom handle in half if I got peeved enough. And I kept growing taller, but Uncle Spade didn't mind so much; he had plans for me:

—I'll tell you when you're ready. . . . In the meantime, kiddo, keep lifting, keep digging, and keep running. Come on, you need to work out, and your uncle's got a thirst after that drive, so get going.

Lynnesha hated him making me go on beer runs. You could

tell by the look in her eye every time he handed me the twenty bucks and walked me to the door. We were staying with her this one time when he sent me out. I was glad to go. It was still sunny when I left her house, but on the way back from Hal's Liquor and Lounge on Alhambra Avenue, it started to rain. I'd just passed the post office with the case under one arm when all of a sudden the sky got gray like ashes. By the time I made it to the tuxedo shop on the corner, all the streetlamps had flickered on. As everybody cleared off the streets, the rain started in waves, so I tucked the case under my T-shirt. Everything got slippery: the case, the sidewalk, my skin. Wind started whipping through the trees. But I didn't stop. I didn't want to hear my uncle yell at me how I couldn't handle a little wet, how he thought I was tougher than that, so I kept going. Cold drops pricked my face and knees. The cardboard case started crumbling under my shirt. Then the air chilled, and I couldn't tell if the prickling was water or ice. Hail grew from peas to Ping-Pong balls, ripping leaves off the trees and denting car hoods. A big nugget hit me on the top of the head and hurt bad. I was running as quick as I could, counting blocks in my head—four left, then three, two—then I could see her house there at the dead end. By then the hail felt like knuckles, knocking my head and shinbones and shoulder blades, making a noise that rang through my ears.

I busted through the door with cans of beer tumbling from

under my shirt, dripping on her floor. Lynnesha hollered at my uncle while he just sat in front of her TV. He picked up a fallen can and cracked it open, shaking his head, chuckling. Lynnesha dried me with towels and walked me to her room, wrapping me in her comforter. I started wheezing.

—That hail and cold must've given you a bug, Lynnesha said to me, and to my uncle, YOU DID THIS, FRANKLIN!

Of course he screamed back, and mostly cusswords I don't want to say:

—Don't tell me how to BLEEPING take care of the kid. You don't know BLEEP. He don't BLEEPING listen to you. You think he'd stay around if he didn't respect his uncle Spade, huh? Huh?

—You better shut that fat mouth of yours, Lynnesha shot back at him, or I'll come in there and shut it. You hear me? Don't say one more word. Not one.

They kept going back and forth and back. She helped me lie down at the foot of her bed. The last thing I heard was Spade slamming the door. Man, that hail did make me pretty sick, 'cause I woke up in the pitch-black, screaming from the piranha dream.

—MA, HELP! MA, HELP ME!

Lynnesha ran back in, bug-eyed. She lifted my head into her lap, smoothing my sweaty hair. My teeth were knocking together, 'cause I was burning up. My skin felt like it could melt plastic. She said she had to get me into the bathtub and helped me off the floor. She couldn't hold me up, and her skinny arms around my waist started shaking, so I stumbled toward the bathroom light and landed on the edge of the tub, falling against the wall. Lynnesha unwrapped me from the sweat-soaked comforter. She swept the shower curtain out of the way and ran the cold water. I was so out of it, I could hardly hold my head up while she peeled off my T-shirt. I stared at her fuzzy sweater. It looked like raspberry sherbet and made me smile through my chattering teeth. Lynnesha told me to take off my underpants, so I slid them down quick and covered my parts with one hand. Then I touched the icy water rushing from the faucet and started mumbling:

—No no no I'm okay I'm okay I'm okay no no no . . .

—Shush, honey, please, she whispered. Slip into the water. We've got to cool you off.

She tried easing me into the tub, but I was like a cat, spreading my arms and legs wide, trying to stay out of the water and forgetting to cover my parts.

—No. NO. NO!

—Shush, Wyatt, she kept whispering, you're going to be fine. We just got to get you in this tub and soak you, cool your skin. It's on fire and you're real sick. Shush now, shush, and stop fighting me, put your legs in, come on now, and your bottom, just slide down slow, slide down, come on now.

I got so weak, she finally pressed me down by the shoulders, then pushed one foot in and the other until my whole body followed. I let out a howl that scared Lynnesha, then made her angry for being scared. All my muscles tightened up and I got goose bumps all over, but I just didn't have the energy to do nothing, except say, No, no, no, and watch this little tiny saint charm on a necklace slip out of her raspberry sweater as she leaned over to rub me with a icy washcloth. I watched the saint swing back and forth as she washed down me, purring:

—Shush, shush, honey, calm now, cool now, Wyatt, that's a good boy . . .

I was just too weak. I let her rub the washcloth over my belly, over my legs and my iceberg knees sticking out of the ocean, then down again, close to my floating parts, up again to my chest and neck and one ear and face and the other ear and then down again. I panted, sharp and quick, watching her pretty face concentrating. She talked quieter and quieter till her voice was just breaths, the only other sound sloshing water from her hand moving down me and up me and down until my eyes closed and my body heat warmed the water and all my goose bumps went away and the washcloth touched my parts and my body sunk into her motion, letting her do what she needed to do while I passed out.

I lay on the couch for two days, and Uncle Spade looked past me like I wasn't there. Lynnesha didn't say nothing. I wanted to tell her something, but I didn't know what to say, and I wanted to talk to my uncle, to have everybody happy. Instead nobody said nothing. We just pretended nothing happened. I got kind of good at that, pretending things never happened.

CHAPTER FIFTEEN

I WAS SO GLAD TO LEAVE

Lynnesha's then and felt bad for feeling that way, but finally I could relax and work hard, practicing my punches, blocks, ducks. I didn't care about the names of the punches I threw. I just knew how to do them real good. I watched prizefights on TV and copied them. Problem was, Uncle Spade gave me weird advice, like:

—Only fight for money, never fight for free.

And he made up answers to most of my questions that didn't help me none. He'd say:

—I don't know, kiddo, just hit the guy hard, REAL HARD. See, one time this fat fool told me I was a liar and threw down his pool cue, waiting for me to rush him. Well, I told him never to call Spade Reaves a liar and backed up a step like I was leaving. Out the corner of my eye, I saw him sit back down and that's when I jumped him quick. No hesitation. And caught him on the chin twice, BAM BAM, both fists, no break, his fat jiggling as he slammed to the floor. He stayed down and I counted me the winner of that game. So don't hesitate, got it?

—But how? Quick like this, ONE-TWO, or like this, POP-POP?

—Dang, Wyatt, listen to what I'm telling you: Just hit the guy hard, REAL HARD.

So that's when he took me to The Gauge Coleman International Gym. Gauge used to be a real fighter, and he had the mashed-in nose to prove it. People said he fought once in Madison Square Garden in New York City and that impressed other people, even though he never won. But no wins made him worth something: made him good for bets. He was a super-old guy with long white sideburns and ropes of muscles under his saggy skin. He didn't smile back at me, but he told my uncle I needed to train with him for at least a year. Uncle Spade said we'd see. Gauge helped me lots. He put me in a real ring, showed me my focus, got me to listen to my muscles, practice their motion, and memorize it. He said it was like dancing.

—I never danced before, I told him.

—Well, you're dancing now, Sharpie.

He always nicknamed folks, 'cause he had a crummy memory. So everybody who came into the gym called me Sharpie.

—Most fighters don't use their real name anyways. They even change it if they get a bad reputation.

—I'll quit if I lose.

He chuckled without smiling. During the training, Gauge didn't talk much. He just watched, his arms crossed over his chest, nodding for good and shaking his head for bad.

I never got to know Gauge Coleman. I don't know if he even liked me, but the weird thing was I felt like he was part of my family, like a cousin maybe or a granddad. I didn't hang out with him except when he was coaching me, and the only time he really talked to me was 'cause I made him mad. This one time, his gym was so packed with people and sweaty-hot, I got slow and sleepy.

—Sharpie, he said. Come here. Let's you and me go outside a minute.

He put his dry, hard hand on my shoulder and guided me downstairs to the parking lot. I figured he was going to holler. What if he hit me? I couldn't hit an old guy back. Instead he rested me up against the brick wall in the shade and handed me the garden hose. I slurped a long time and waited, knowing he was going to talk. That kind of waiting can drag on forever. Finally, as I put the hose above my head and cooled down, my brain catching up with the rest of me, Gauge Coleman sucked air through his teeth and chuckled, saying:

—Kid, there's a lot you are going to have to learn, and it's not just muscles, no matter what people tell you. No matter what your uncle says, it isn't all muscle. The world is built on a balance of strength and smarts, so you have to learn that connection, Sharpie. You don't need schoolbooks necessarily, but you do need to listen to what's going on in your brain. You feel slow in the head, how are your muscles going to react? See? If you're thinking about tomorrow and not right now, then how are your feet going to know where they go? See?

—Kind of. I guess, I said, smiling.

—You're not even using your brain right now, are you?

—I'm trying, but—

—Jeez. You're still such a kid. No trying. Do it. Listen to me. Too many people let words into their head and then let them slip right out the other side.

I tried to get it. I closed my eyes and moved my feet, feeling what was in my brain, but it was like thinking about breathing.

—It ain't easy to think and move, I told him.

He chuckled at me, leaning back on the hood of a old station wagon, saying:

—But that's the challenge, Sharpie: You gotta be able to do both, think and move, not just move. Smart fighting . . .

That was where I thought he was wrong. I could never figure out how he wanted me to do both. For me, fighting was about not thinking. So sometimes I'd just squinch up my eyebrows so he'd see the thinking going on, and then I continued to listen to my bones and skin and muscles, 'cause I didn't want to dis-respect him.

Maybe a couple weeks later, I was getting in some sit-ups when Gauge came up, standing over me, arms crossed like usual. He told me to do twenty more, then we'd get cracking.

—And Wyatt, he added, looking down over his arms. Listen. I don't want your uncle selling around the gym no more.

—Selling what?

—Don't matter what. I don't want him selling. You tell him.

Fortunately, I didn't have to. When I took a break, Uncle Spade was standing at the water cooler. He waved me over, grinning like crazy.

—Wyatt, kiddo, good news. I got you your first fight. I gotta work out a couple things first, so I'm heading out. You stay here, keep working with Coleman, and I'll be back tomorrow.

—You're leaving me here alone? I asked, his shiny sun-glasses reflecting my shoulders and head back at me.

—You can handle it, he said. It's just one night. I'll be here in the morning.

—Okay.

I grinned back at him and nodded. I could stay at the motel by myself, my first time alone since my last night in Fever and Ma's house. I guess it was a reward for my first fight, and besides, I was a big kid now. Uncle Spade slapped me on the shoulder.

—IT'S STARTING! He chuckled. Can you believe it, man? We're gonna be rich.

I stayed up late that night, the TV on, a bag of chips and three cans of root beer for supper. My first night alone and I wanted it to be kind of special. Instead it was a regular night: me falling asleep and waking to the TV flickering and the whole world shut down.

CHAPTER SIXTEEN

UNCLE SPADE ALWAYS
called it "boxing," but what I did was fight. Fist fight. I had
gloves from Gauge Coleman, but we made more money without them. Crowds like a real knockdown show with blood and
bruises. There wasn't no ring like in the matches I'd watched.
And no ref. No rounds. And no mats, bleachers, seats, or bells.
It was usually a back room or basement with a plain cement
floor and crates for sitting. But sometimes there wasn't even
that. Not even a room. Like my first fight, out back of Larry's
shop stacked with used tires. The building didn't even have a
back door. You had to walk around the side and through a high
chain-link fence topped in barbed wire. And after the sun went
down, that dirt yard surrounded by high-stacked radials felt
like a black room. A old rusted Firebird, half worked on, half

rusted away, sat on cement blocks by the building wall. One streetlight curved down over the car.

That fight went good enough, I guess. I mean, I won. But I didn't enjoy it too much. The day before, my uncle'd made the final plans for me to take on one of Larry's workers. Then he made the rounds, mentioning the fight to certain men. He made each guy feel important. Not just anybody was allowed to bet.

—You gotta keep this quiet, he whispered in their ears. All right?

But that was a lie. Larry had invited the sheriff, since their girls played softball together. The fight wouldn't start till the men'd finished supper at home and found a way out of the house on a Tuesday night. I thought it was weird to have it on a Tuesday. I thought my first fight should've been on a weekend. I also figured it should have been in a ring. But the men came, just like my uncle said they would.

—Pick a small enough town and the guys'll show up for any kind of entertainment, especially if they can make some cash off a pal.

That morning, while my uncle was out making the rounds, I did exactly what he told me. First I ran along the river where the sand met the grass. Then I asked a old guy if he needed help in his yard and told him I'd do it for free. After I finished digging him his hole, I found a jungle gym in a park for my pull-ups and did a final beer run for Uncle Spade. With the

leftover money, I ate. I polished off two omelets with cheese
and a burger. I also drank two chocolate shakes and three big
pops and had a hot fudge sundae for dessert, then went back
to the motel to lay down. As I stretched out under the air con-
ditioner in my underpants, I heard a knock at the window. I
sat up and listened. My belly was so stuffed, I didn't want to
get off the floor to see who it was. Partly, too, I knew something was wrong. Sometimes you just know. Besides, who
knocks just once? I wiped the sweat off my face and sighed,
then dragged myself up.

The sun bit my eyes as I opened the spring-loaded door.
Heat waffled up my legs and tummy. I made my hand into
a shade and checked, but nobody was outside. Something
crinkled in the dry weeds under the window, and my stomach
twisted up like when you get spun to hit a piñata. I jammed my
shoe in the doorway to keep it from locking me out, then knelt
down and spread the brown weeds careful, ready to jump back.
There lay a mini brown bird, shaking, its neck crooked and
beak opened up like a yawn. All my skin prickled when I figured
it'd slammed into the glass. It was tinier than a eight ball. Just
picking it up, I thought I might pinch it in two. When I cupped
it with both hands and took it into the air-conditioned room,
it peeped and shivered, or twitched maybe. I couldn't tell. Its
feathers were thin and missing in spots where you could see
raw, red skin. Maybe it was young. Maybe it was learning to fly.

I pressed my finger against its neck, light as I could, trying to straighten it out. It chirped sharp, so I stopped. I didn't know what to do. I didn't know the first thing about birds. I knew they made nests. How could I help? What if I fed it a aspirin? I could grind it up. Mix it in water, even. How about tying a popsicle stick to its neck to keep it straight?

I pet it with one finger, but the feathers weren't soft like I figured. Red swam on the surface of its eye, and it wouldn't stop shaking. The bird was going to die. It didn't need to lay there hurting. It needed to die. How could I do it? Quick and painless. Electricity? No. Pillow? No. Toilet? No. I needed to be smarter. I wasn't smart enough to figure out the right answer. I needed somebody smart to help, but I was alone.

I decided to first lay him on a washcloth for comfort. With one quick motion, I flipped him into the white cloth. Bird blood speckled my palm. I wiped it on my underpants, making stains like comets, dots with little tails. My mouth watered. I thought I was going to puke, but I kept it down. I needed somebody to help, somebody who knew birds. I reached for the phone but stopped. There was nobody. My uncle wouldn't care. He'd probably laugh at me for being a sissy. Besides, he was too busy out advertising my fight. So who would care? If only there was some kind of doctor for birds or a hospital, I'd have taken him.

Instead I made a plan all by myself. I carried him in the

washcloth around the back of the motel, grabbing a cement block from under the drain spout. One piece of advice I know: If you don't like something, don't think about it. Turn your head off. I'd been practicing that a lot and getting good at it. Cool air hung in the low tree branches. The dirt smelled wet and rotten. I laid the washcloth down and folded the edges over, covering up his squirming little body. Then I raised the block over my head. Gravel crumbled off from my tight grip. *Head off*, I told myself. *Stay off. Stay off.* . . . My hands got steady and I brought the block down. It made a flat thud.

I squatted down next to the gray block and scraped leaves away until I had a bare spot. Then I rammed my fingers in, putting my whole body into digging a deep hole. The dirt dug under my fingernails. It was getting late. I could barely see my hands. I lifted the block and slid the red washcloth in, then filled the hole and stomped the dirt flat with my bare feet. On my way back to the room to wait for Uncle Spade, I put the block back in its spot. Head off.

CHAPTER SEVENTEEN

—WHY'RE YOU MUDDY?

Uncle Spade asked when he walked in. And why're you naked,
Wyatt? You gotta get ready for tonight, kiddo. Shake off those
jitters. COME ON!

—My head's off, I mumbled.

—WELL, FLIP IT ON, MAN, AND LET'S GET GOING, he
said, spinning me around and walking into the bathroom.
Washing up, I could hear him talking on the phone, quiet and
cussing like he used to fight with Fever, but I just shoved my
head under water so I didn't have to listen.

When we got to Larry's Tire Shop, my uncle couldn't stop
smoking like crazy and running his hands through his hair. He
talked to everybody, while I sat on a stack of tires, watching
people file in, trying to figure out which one I was fighting.

Crickets hid in the tires and took turns calling out. Flies spun around the one lightbulb while I stretched. When Larry announced he'd be collecting bets, people turned to look me over. *Take a look*, I thought, *I don't care.*

—How you doing? You okay? my uncle asked, a grin spread thick on his face.

—Fine, I said, not smiling.

—You need to stretch. Did you stretch?

—Yes.

—What do you need? Water? You ready to do this? You nervous?

—I need quiet.

—Okay. All right. I'll give you that. You just make sure you're limber and focused. You can take this little man. I let Flint know you're just a teenager.

—Who's Flint?

—The one you're fighting. He's over there, in the greasy green jumpsuit. He figures you're only nineteen. Thinks he can take you easy.

—I need quiet.

—Don't be nervous, kiddo. You can do it. Remember, block your—

—Uncle Spade. Please . . .

He dropped his head and sucked in a breath, not wanting to flip out on me and knowing I was about to flip out on him. I felt this power with nothing in my brain—no caring, no thinking, no words—just the bird, and I had no doubt I'd destroy that man across from me taping his knuckles.

Larry stepped into the circle of light, his hair shiny and long like spaghetti, but with none on top. He had money fanning out between his knuckles and waving as he talked:

—As most of you know, Flint here's one of my best buds and a dang fine worker, even if he has started enough bar brawls to put most of town in the hospital at one time or another. Finally he's putting his fighting to good use.

Everybody chuckled real low. I breathed in the tire rubber and beer, holding the air in and staring at Flint. He was a full foot shorter than me and bald. A scar ran from one big ear to the edge of his eye. He was staring back, rubbing both fists together.

—TONIGHT, Larry yelled, dabbing sweat off his face, fighting Flint for your enjoyment, we got young Wyatt Reaves, who looks a little rambunctious to me. This here's his first fight, but I'm sure he'll do his best. . . .

The circle of guys laughed and shook their heads.

—*That*, my uncle had told me, *is the advantage we got. They'll mistake your being young for weakness. Then you'll pound him into the ground.*

Larry winked at a couple of his pals near the front as they stomped out their smokes, ready to watch. Then he turned around real slow and said:

—So let's get to it. Everybody know the rules? And this time, Pete, keep out of their way. Let 'em go till one stays down.

Larry pulled Flint to his side. I took off my sweatshirt and stood up. My uncle set his hand on the flat of my back, guiding me into the circle. The crowd backed into the shadows, giving us space. Uncle Spade's hand pulled away and left a cool spot. Then Larry asked if we were ready. I hooked eyes with Flint, the bird with its crooked neck floating in the air between us. We both nodded. All my skin warmed, numbed. I raised one fist to protect my chin and waited for him to hit me. I wanted to feel it. None of the coaching, the footwork, or the ring practice was there. Just my skin and bone knowing what to do, needing him to swing first.

A small, sure smile smeared his lips. He faked a right and jabbed with his left, clipping my cheek. I let it connect. It was surprising how little it hurt at first—just a bug bite. My neck jerked back, then the sting spread across that side of my face. He shook his fist a little. It hurt him more than me. The burn woke my skin and widened my eyes. My fists started to work. My feet danced their dance with the little drag on the ground to keep them in the circle. My left shot into his stomach and he tried not to double over. His eyes shrunk. Man, he was mad. And he started punching mad, but I blocked each one. No crowd or cricket, shuffle, grunt, or clap, just the sound of breathing filled my ears. And the sight of that bloody bird set right between his eyes. That's when everything packed into the points of my knuckles aimed to break his nose. The soft bone bent on my fist, then snapped. My left followed—Flint was too surprised by the break to block. I clipped his chin, tilting him back like he was lying in bed midair. Then he dropped, skin scraping the ground, head smacking, bouncing twice. The pain in my knuckles shot down into my wrist and crammed in, curling up there as I watched his eyes roll back. His arm raised up, twitched, and fell.

Sweat got in my eyes and burned, so I closed them and waited for Spade to bring me a towel and my sweatshirt. That dang bird still floated on the back of my eyelids while hands slapped my arms and shoulder.

—YOU DID IT, MAN! my uncle shouted in my ear. YOU FREAKING TOOK HIM OUT! I KNEW YOU COULD, WYATT! DIDN'T I TELL YOU?

His hands tightened around my biceps as he walked me to the pile of tires.

—Sit down, he said. I gotta collect. I'll be back. I gotta collect.

I felt around with my right hand for my sweatshirt, my left not working too good, still holding in the pain. I patted my eyes until the burn stopped and then opened them to the crowd around Flint. He was still down. Larry took turns holding a towel to his friend's head and passing out the cash. Looked like he had a lot to hand out. My uncle was talking to the sheriff, with a grin so big his mustache straightened out and made him look silly. I remembered that little smile Flint snuck me when we'd started, like he was better than me, and it made me glad I'd dumped the guy.

Crickets in the tire stacks started calling again as people disappeared in the darkness. Uncle Spade helped Larry carry Flint's dangling body into the shop, then came back to count the winnings. He sat on a tire next to me. It sloshed with water inside. I pulled my sweatshirt over my head with one hand, smearing the blood from my lip.

—Dang it. Blood on my sweatshirt, I grumbled.

—You're okay. I'll get you a new one, kiddo, MY KIDDO. Jeez, you're amazing. They never expected that from you. They were joking around, and now they're dragging their sorry butts home with no lunch money. Why? Because it's right here in MY HAND!

—How much? I asked, smiling big.

—I'm counting. I'm counting . . . and eighty-five. Hold on one second. . . .

He smoothed the bills out on his leg from a crumpled fist-ful. Larry came out carrying a small metal box. He smiled at me and told me I'd done good, real good, and here was my hundred bucks. He swung open the box and took out one crisp bill. He told us Flint was doing fine, but he was going for some more ice, and did I need any?

—No, thank you, I said, looking at the bill.

—We are going to live THE GOOD LIFE. Yes, we are. Let's get you some food. Wings and a chocolate shake. How 'bout that? How 'bout ten shakes? And a thousand wings, huh?

—Uncle Spade, I think I need to go to the hospital.

My wrist was broke. I'd punched wrong. I didn't really get what the doctor explained. Something about the angle of the punch and keeping my wrist straight the next time. He hoped there wouldn't be a next time. Thought I got in a fight at school, my being only . . . what, fifteen? A kid had cornered me by the bike racks and wouldn't let me go, so I had to defend myself. That's what Uncle Spade explained, paying for my cast and painkillers with some bet money.

—We'll get that thing off, my uncle said, helping me into the Chevy. Don't you worry. We'll get you fighting again real soon. Now it's party time. Think you're up for some beers?

Uncle Spade tucked a napkin in my sweatshirt for me. Gosh, we ate wings till our bellies bit our belts. It was so good. I chugged my milkshake so fast I got brain freeze. We laughed at how hard it was for me to eat with my right hand, dropping food on my jeans. Uncle Spade just couldn't stop grinning. I grinned too, through the throbbing, the drugs making my eyes go fuzzy.

CHAPTER EIGHTEEN

WHEN I TURNED FIFTEEN

for real, Spade threw me a birthday party. It was the best one I ever had—and the first. It was the best, 'cause I felt like the people there kind of liked me and wanted to spend time with me and maybe life might turn out okay. I remember most of that night, but not all of it, 'cause it was also the first time I'd ever drunk alcohol.

This is how. I remember the Gentlemen's Club where Lynnesha worked, with all the men in suits and all the ladies wearing a heck of a lot less. I remember Lynnesha carrying a tray covered in glasses of booze. And I remember Uncle Spade and me both wearing club-owned sport coats and sitting at a big table with a RESERVED sign. I remember fuzzy curtains and giganto naked-lady paintings covering the walls. And I remember Uncle Spade leaning over and clinking his bourbon against my something-sunrise, saying:

—Man, get ready, Wyatt. Here's your big bad birthday surprise.

And that's when Lynnesha's friend, Jeanie, threw back one of the curtains, tossing dust into the lights, and stepped out in a teeny-weeny policeman uniform, making all the guys cheer. I tried to keep my mouth shut. She was the last thing I expected. I thought maybe a magician or a clown or something, not a lady too old for a Halloween costume twitching and bobbing like she was all by herself. I sipped my pretty drink and shuddered. A steely cough-syrup taste snuck through the roof of my mouth and up behind my eyes, warming my brain. Jeanie straddled a black chair and made a funny squeal like a nail stuck her.

—Pretty dang hot, huh? Spade said, setting his arm on my shoulders.

I jumped at his touch, nodding, not quite sure what to say. Instead I just kept sipping my sunrise thing, my body starting to feel soft. My uncle had relaxed too. I could see it in his eyes. Other ladies danced: a schoolteacher and a devil, and as each one finished her shift, they joined us, giving me birthday pecks on the cheek.

When Mittens Holiday finally got on stage, the room was pretty empty. I'd had maybe four drinks and was surrounded by beautiful ladies who couldn't get over how cute and big I was.

I kept wrapping my arms around them and squeezing, probably too tight. My eyes got blurry, me thinking 'cause it was way past bedtime. Mittens was this big lady with too much hair who swooped in with her microphone and a long, flowy dress.

—Happy birthday, big boy, she said, and people started laughing.

I stood up, knocking the table and spilling drinks.

—I have a cast on my arm, I said, my tongue fumbling.

—Oh my, you're eager. Come let your auntie give you a big wet birthday smooch.

More laughs as I scooted around the table. Spade swiped at the back of my jacket, knocking over my chair. Mittens grabbed me under one arm and yanked me up on stage.

—Ooo, baby doll, you're big and beefy as a trucker. Are you a trucker?

—No, I said. I ain't no trucker, I'm a—

—Sure, dearie. You're anything you want to be, she cooed, and then said to the audience, Including a teensy bit tipsy.

The others roared, and I didn't realize I was the joke. The girls all called out to me, their words scrambled. I still turn red thinking about it. I knew Mittens was making fun of me, but at the same time she made me feel like maybe I was *her* nephew too.

—Now, give Auntie Mittens a little birthday peck.

Everybody was shouting NO. I leaned forward and puckered

my lips. She leaned her cheek toward me, and just as she got next to my lips, she turned and gave me a big wet open-mouth kiss. I jerked back.

—Why'd you do that? I yelped.

Two guys hollered and jeered. The girls squealed, and I laughed with them. Mittens helped me down off the stage and thanked me for the time of her life. As I fell into my chair, Uncle Spade gripped my arm and bumped his lips against my ear.

—You freaking idiot. That's a guy in girl's clothes. Wipe that lipstick off your mouth.

I pulled away and looked at him to see if he was joking, but he wasn't. I rubbed my mouth with the back of my fist. I felt bad, but the girls saved me; they moved in closer and tousled my hair and ran their hands over my face and each planted a kiss on my lips. Finally, Spade chuckled and said:

—Now that's more like it.

It's funny how things just happen and suddenly you can say, I know how to drink or smoke or fight or whistle, or I know what it's like to kiss a guy. Then if somebody asks if you know, you have to decide to tell the truth or a lie.

Mittens finished singing some songs. The room spun with the faces of the ladies and Lynnesha and Spade and the ladies again, their words licking my ears like a slobbering dog, everybody talking and drinking and who's got a car and was Mittens coming and who's that and watch what Wyatt drinks 'cause you know what'll happen, ha ha ha, somebody grab his arm.

We were all outside in the parking lot, a cool wind clearing my eyes a little, so I could see a new lady. She had paper clips dangling from her ears and a bald head, and she leaned against her convertible, a cigarette hanging out her mouth. We all piled in and I didn't worry about none of it, 'cause the alcohol doesn't really let you worry. The bald lady drove with the roof down, Lynnesha and Spade up front next to her, city noises booming, streetlights swooshing past, and the stars staying still.

—IT'S MY BIRTHDAY! I hollered at her through the wind.

—CONGRATS, she said, sticking her hand over the seat for me to shake.

I couldn't believe I was surrounded by all those great people partying just for me. They were my friends, I thought right then, the nicest, best friends I'd ever had. Then the next thing I remember, we were all in a shop. Bright white lights flickered on, making everybody squint, and making Spade cuss. It felt like a doctor's office but looked like a circus, drawings all over the wall. One lady flipped on the stereo. Bottles got pulled out of bags and cigars got lit, while I wavered like a tree in the wind, my dry mouth hanging open.

I watched the bald lady wipe down a dentist chair she had behind the counter. She still didn't smile, like Spade. I couldn't stop staring at her. Something made my heart chug.

I didn't start getting it till Spade blew a long stream of smoke and said:

—Kiddo, you take a good look at those walls. Find one you like.

I walked around with my nose close to each heart wrapped in thorns, bulldog, rose, and angel while my head was talking to my stomach: Stay down . . . stay down . . . , it said.

Uncle Spade walked me over to the bald lady. Keeping his hand on my back, he said:

—Wyatt, you wanna get inked? Smudge here is the best.

The truth was, I'd never even thought about tattoos before. Did he really want me to do this? That was all I cared about. Would this make me more his? Would it make him happy? But all that got messed up in my head, and I looked into his eyes as best I could and nodded, and Spade turned to the ladies, shouting:

—HE'S DOING IT!

They all cheered, saying I was going to look so tough, be so cool, be a real man. Smudge turned to me to explain her trademark style. She used a razor blade and black ink. It had to go fast, and I had to be sure of what I wanted.

—I want a piranha. You know what—what that is?

—Yeah, I can do that, she said, grabbing a sketchpad and scribbling. Like that?

She'd drawn the exact fish from my dream, with huge teeth

like house nails and scales like small knives, like it was coming at me, eating me down to bones. I don't know how I thought that up, but all of it, the whole night, felt like a dream. Smudge yanked off my shirt and dropped my drunk body into the dentist chair. One lady tickled me and giggled in my ear:

—Big strong baby boy . . . so manly, baby . . . yes, you are, yes . . .

The booze was so far under my skin I couldn't stop her from talking at me like I was a kitten. She was the one who'd wake up next to me in the morning on Lynnesha's floor. Then everybody gathered around the chair to sing the "Happy Birthday to Wyatt" song. All the words sounded like mashed potatoes, but I loved it, until Smudge made them go away.

—I'm putting this where you can decide who sees it and who doesn't, okay?

I just grinned at her, focusing my eyes on the earring in her nose. She unbuttoned my pants and pealed them back a bit, then wiped alcohol on the spot to the right of my belly button, below my hip bone.

—You move, Wyatt, and I'll mess up. Don't even flinch, she explained. I'm doing this as a favor to Spade. Anybody asks you, I didn't tag you. Okay?

She dipped a razor blade in alcohol and leaned over me. I clenched up my stomach and breathed real low. Smudge cut me quick, then dipped her thumb in black ink and smeared it across the cut. Then, with her other hand, she wiped the extra off and cut again. I didn't feel much. Sure didn't hurt like breaking my wrist. It was quick and smooth in big motions.

—Doing good, Wyatt, Smudge said. Not many can take it.

I couldn't talk or close my dizzy eyes, so I listened through the girls' noises and the music to Smudge talking, not hearing her words, till she said just one:

—There.

Uncle Spade leaned over my face, his eyes all glassy, and said:

—Dang, kiddo. You're tough as nails. Even I ain't had the guts to get that done. Man, you're gonna scare them right out of the ring. . . .

I grinned at him like a idiot as he swayed away. Lynnesha rubbed my shoulder and wiped the sweat off my forehead, slurring:

—It's all right, sugar, it's all done. Everything's going to be fine.

CHAPTER NINETEEN

IT WASN'T SO BAD HAVING

a broke wrist. Worst part was Uncle Spade drinking and fighting, waiting for me to get back in action. The best part of that time was sleeping on the flat roof of Hubcap Sandy's repair shop. As always, Sandy got the Chevy purring like a tiger. It took a week, waiting for parts and all (but I think she slowed down the fixing to keep Uncle Spade around). Every night after dark, I'd slide out her back window with a air mattress and climb up the rusted fire escape to the roof. I liked watching the stars till I fell asleep. Soon as the Chevy worked, we were off to sell some cases of rug cleaner. On the drive, I thought about Lynnesha and told Uncle Spade how I was kind of missing her.

—You trying to take my ladyfriend? he said, laughing, making me turn red.

But as quick as the cleaner was sold, we ended up back at her place and sort of almost settled in. Uncle Spade had figured out his perfect merchandise: Funny T-shirts he and Bad Back Jack found at this fire sale held in the end of the warehouse that didn't burn. Jack was visiting from the City. He was off drugs and only smoked pot. He drove Uncle Spade in his pickup out past the oatmeal factory to load up the shirts. I couldn't go 'cause of my cast.

Lynnesha didn't mind so much anymore when Uncle Spade left me at her place. He'd take off with the shirts and come back every couple days. There wasn't much yelling, and me and Lynnesha spent lots of time together. We got into a regular way of life, her and me making dinner each night before she had to go to work.

Most days, us two just sat in her backyard and talked. She used me for all the listening Spade refused to do, teaching me how to make virgin raspberry margaritas and not teasing me about them being girly drinks. She showed me how to coat the rim of a glass with sugar by wetting it first. I'd carry the blender with my good hand. She'd bring out the lawn chairs and radio. I remember one day real good. It was one of those perfect afternoons when the heat and sun warm your skin just right. One of those times you think about later when you need something to remind you how life can be. It was quiet and slow. The sky looked like a lake, and if you listened carefully between sips you could hear the train whistles down at the yard. Just me and Lynnesha with nothing to do except hang laundry. We took turns saying stuff we just thought up, like I said:

—It feels good being barefoot out here with you.

And she said:

—Sure does.

—I'm taking my shirt off, I said.

—Okay, she said, squinting at me, making her high cheeks higher.

I pulled the back of my collar over my head.

—The sun feels good, I said. Hey, do you get sunburn?

—If I'm out for hours, she said.

—I like it if it's not too bad.

—Sunburn?

—Yeah. I like pushing my finger on it and I like that crinkly warm feeling you get and I like taking cold showers afterward.

Lynnesha laughed, picking a wood clip from the basket.

—What? I asked.

—You.

—Me, what?

—Just you, she said, folding cloth over the rope and clipping it down.

Lynnesha disappeared behind the blowing bedsheet and her shadow spread into slices, only her legs showing. I unknotted two T-shirts, then flapped out the wrinkles and extra water like she showed me. I closed my eyes to the spray coating my chest and face, then licked the mist off my upper lip and listened to the sheets.

—Do you have other boyfriends? I asked. Besides my uncle?

—Wyatt . . . , she said, pulling the sheet aside.

—Okay. I know. No nosing, I said, batting at the sheet with my cast.

—It's not that. It's just silly for you to ask. Your uncle is my guy, but—

—But when he's gone, who knows how long he'll be.

—Like right now. Where'd he go?

—To sell T-shirts in Dubuque.

—Or Des Moines or Dallas or Downer's Grove. He says he's going to Dubuque, but, well, you've been with him. You know how it goes.

—He'll be back tomorrow. He said he would.

—Yes, he did say he would. But then how long will you two stay?

—Maybe we ain't leaving.

—Hand me that pair of pants.

I flapped the jeans and sprayed her with water. She snatched them from my hands, smiling, and wiped her eyes. I lay down in the grass and watched a bird spinning in the air, catching bugs. The grass was cool on my back. I wiggled my arms and legs. Lynnesha hooked the empty laundry basket on her hip and wandered to the back steps, where she'd left her margarita and a bottle of tequila. I was thirsty, but the grass felt too good to get up.

—I can't stop smiling, I said up to the sky.

—Why?

—I don't know. . . . Sometimes you forget how good a smile can feel. . . .

—But sometimes it's work to keep smiling, she said, running the cool glass along her neck.

—Uncle Spade doesn't smile much.

—No, he does not.

—I only remember Fever smiling once, I said, rolling onto my side and looking at her through the grass blades.

—Who?

—Fever's what I call my dad.

—Your dad? I never heard you—

—It was a funny day a long time ago, the day he smiled. I was maybe only eight.

—Wyatt?

—What?

—No, go ahead. I'm listening. Tell me.

So I told her how that afternoon I lined up my whole bucket of army men and aimed them one by one at the front door so when Fever came home he'd get shot dead. Millions of tiny green plastic bullets and hand grenades and missiles would slam him. I could hardly stand the wait. It got late and Ma fell asleep on her couch, but finally Fever kicked the front door open and that smile stopped the bullets. He was happy, and for first time, I saw him really grin ear to ear.

—I WON, he shouted. I'M RICH!

My army men got snapped in half under his feet. Ma startled up, pulling her robe shut, and glared at Fever, but that smile flooded the room. His red-faced bar buddies stumbled in behind him, and he flipped on a Elvis record so loud the speakers thumped.

—FIVE HUNDRED DOLLARS, he hollered, tossing Ma a beer.

The other guys stepped over me and dropped their six-packs in a pile on the table. Everybody above me filled the room, their shoulders brushing the walls. Elvis started speeding things up. Fever yanked Ma into his arms and they bumped their beers together. As he spun her into a dance, he pulled the cash from his pocket and rubbed it across her chest. That's when Fever looked down to see me. His big teeth shined out from his thick black beard, his eyes glassy and red. Still keeping Ma moving, he dropped a twenty. It floated, flipping into my open palms, and when it landed, he said:

—There you go, Wyatt. Don't say I never gave you nothing, kiddo!

Lynnesha looked me in the eyes. I stared back and said:

—I think it's crazy you can forget how you feel about somebody from one second to the next, and you hope that feeling stays around forever, forgetting your army men until the next morning when you get yelled at for the mess.

—Oh, Wyatt, you are such a sweet boy.

That made me blush, so I walked to her and turned my back. She wiped the grass off with both hands, then I pulled my shirt back on and sighed.

—I wish I could live with you for always.

—Oh no, sweetie. I could never raise a child, she said, laughing lightly as if what she said was no big deal, then stepped inside to make lunch.

CHAPTER TWENTY

UNCLE SPADE CAME BACK
early from Downer's Grove. It hadn't gone too good, but he
decided he'd take the eight leftover boxes to university towns,
'cause those stupid college kids would buy anything. That night
the three of us counted T-shirts. We sat on the floor in Lynnesha's living room with our glasses of pop next to us and the
TV off, each taking a box and opening it, checking the shirts for
burns, then separating them by logo.

—I got ten 'I'M WITH STUPID's in this box, I said.

—Here, add them to my pile, Lynnesha told me, putting out
her arms.

Uncle Spade opened another box for me and told us that Bad
Back Jack bought four boxes off him before he went back to the
City. Lynnesha said:

—Good.

—I'm just glad I got the living room back again, I said.

And they laughed. Grunting, Uncle Spade pulled himself up with the couch arm and went to the kitchen. Lynnesha held up a I'M WITH STUPID T-shirt so the finger pointed at me. I pushed her and she laughed. Uncle Spade plopped down with his glass full of pop.

—Thanks for offering, Lynnesha said, taking it from him and sipping.

—Yeah, thanks for offering, I said.

—We need to wash all these. They still smell like smoke. Tomorrow you two got to wash all of them.

—Yes, sir! she said, saluting.

—Yes, sir! I said, copying her.

—Don't mix the colors. And bleach the whites. Got it?

Me and Lynnesha laughed at him. He shoved her and shot me a look. Through the edge of his mouth he said:

—Keep counting, you two. . . .

He tore open another box, telling us again how finding stupid college students would get them sold in two days, tops. It was his best plan ever. He wished he had more T-shirts.

—I want to go back to school, I said before really thinking.

—You what? Uncle Spade chuckled. Shut up, Wyatt.

—He's serious, Lynnesha said, looking in my eyes.

—Well, Uncle Spade said, that . . . could happen. . . . Till your wrist is strong again, I guess. Least it'd keep you out of my hair. . . . School, huh?

—Yeah, I said, and we'll stay here for a while and you can travel like maybe a day or two and I can stay with Lynnesha and she'll work while I'm asleep and I'd stay out of trouble and study and maybe make some friends.

—I don't know, Uncle Spade said, running his fingers over his mustache.

—Tomorrow morning, Lynnesha said, and folded a shirt, you two should go check it out.

—Yeah, I said, smiling so big, about to explode, and then I'll come back and I'll wash ALL your T-shirts so you can sell them to those stupid college kids, those idiots. . . .

The last time I'd thought about school was back when I was hanging out with my best friend, Clark, and that didn't go too good. The visits when Clark had school, I messed around by myself, staying out of people's way. But at four o'clock, I'd wait on the edge of the woods with a good view of the road where the yellow bus dropped off the three or four pudgy trailer-park girls and Clark, who'd race to meet me at the trees, backpack dragging in the dirt.

—WYATT! Guess what we did today? Clark'd holler, his glasses hopping up and down.

Panting, he'd tell me about whirling science projects and geography films and playing floor hockey. He had a house key hooked to his knapsack zipper. On sunny days, we'd drop off his books and grab handfuls of cookies, then run outside. On rainy days, him and me played in Clark's very own room. I remembered having my own room and kind of missed it. His only fit his bed and a desk made out of old planks by his step-dad. Under his bed he'd hid stacks of comic books. Some-times, him and me, we'd read them together, Clark explaining the important histories while I looked at each bright-colored box. And this one time I was laying on his bed, reading a spe-cial edition *Incredible Hulk* while Clark did homework, when he dropped his pencil, pushed up his glasses, and asked me why I didn't go to school.

—'Cause you're puny, I told him, and kept my eyes on Bruce Banner.

—Come with me, he said. You could keep all the mean kids away and I could help you—

—I can't. I gotta help my uncle with the business.

I stood up, the special edition flapping to the floor, nervous just thinking about it.

—Maybe you could come sometimes, Clark begged. Please, Wyatt. . . .

—Nope. Can't do it, I said, standing in his doorway, kicking at the frame.

And then I walked out, into the woods, my thumb rubbing my piece of Nana glass, trying not to think, mad that he made me.

But this time was different with Spade not traveling so much, you know? I leaned back against the couch, and we all laughed. Even Uncle Spade felt good right then. You could see it on his face. But it's easy to get carried away, thinking everything's okay.

CHAPTER TWENTY-ONE

WE HAD TO DRIVE AROUND

a while to find the school. We'd passed it before but never paid attention. I wore my tie, and Uncle Spade wore his black jeans. On the front door a poster announced: VOTE FOR BOBCAT BEST & WORST TODAY! BALLOTS AT LUNCH! HURRY! HURRY!

I read each sign we passed, sunlight shooting off the empty hallway floor into our eyes:

ROOM 24: SCIENCE LAB

Our shoes clacked loud.

ROOM 22: MR. ROLLINS

Everything was painted the same tan color.

RESTROOMS →

Combination locks on every locker.

OFFICE →

We followed that sign. I wondered if Clark's school looked like this one and wished he was here. Outside the office door, boys lined two wood benches. I smiled at them, but they didn't look up. Suddenly I needed to pee real bad. I'd forgot what school was like: that quiet and that smell. I couldn't go to school. What was I thinking? I'd been away too long. And besides, by then I'd gotten too stupid.

Uncle Spade sniffed and grunted.

—Chalk, he said, and shook his head.

MRS. BENSON had a metal nameplate on her counter. She was a roly-poly lady with nails too long to pick stuff up. She smiled and blinked too much and said to Uncle Spade:

—Yes?

—I want to put my kid in school.

—All right, she said, dragging the words out really long, carefully fingering clipboarded papers from under her counter. Have a seat and fill these out. I'll let Principal Stinson know you're here.

We sat on a bench under a row of more posters: WHO'S BEST DRESSED? MOST HUGGABLE? MOST LIKELY TO GO TO JAIL? SENIORS, GET YOUR VOTES IN!

Uncle Spade's face looked like I felt: caught and sent to the principal's office.

—I hate the smell of chalk too, I whispered.

—What's your social security number? he whispered, side-looking at me.

—My what?

I rubbed my piece of Nana glass in my pocket.

—Wyatt, what the—? Your social security number. You gotta know.

—I don't.

He made up a number and scribbled in Lynnesha's address for mine, leaving most of the other lines blank. Two kids darted in the door and asked for the equipment room key for Coach Liam, then dashed back out. Uncle Spade signed the bottom and handed it back to Mrs. Benson, who looked it over, her eyebrows raising up. Pretty soon she waved those rainbow fingernails toward Principal Stinson's office, and all I could do was think about running. Was I crazy? I had the easy life riding around the country with no hard brain work. And now I was going to screw that up. My forehead got pasty. The skinny principal asked us to have a seat while he reviewed the forms. He looked too young to be gray.

—Mr. Reaves, your son's last school?

—Yeah, um, he said, waving a hand in the air. Don't worry about all that other stuff. We just want to start him out now. That's all.

—But we do worry, Principal Stinson said, leaning toward us, his bony hands smoothing out my papers. It's important that we know who we are dealing with to best help our students start off on the right foot. You understand, don't you? So we'll need to contact his previous school for his records. We'll need his immunization card and, of course, his birth certificate. . . . It is fantastic you're getting such a head start. Now, were you planning on summer school or just registering for next fall?

—Fall? No, we want him to start today.

—Sir, I'm afraid there are only five weeks left of this school year, the principal said, moving his eyes onto me.

I made myself keep smiling, never feeling any dumber in my whole life. I just wanted to take Uncle Spade's arm and drag him out before we got laughed at.

—Man, you people make this stuff too dang hard, Uncle Spade said. Let me have that sheet back.

—Pardon me?

—I SAID, give me that sheet of paper back. Forget it. He don't need this school.

—Mr. Reaves, please. We just need additional information. There's nothing wrong.

Uncle Spade yanked the sheet out of his hand and headed out

the door. I followed. The principal called to us and then asked Mrs. Benson to keep us there, but we kept on walking. Now all the benched kids looked up. Out in the hallway, Uncle Spade let loose a list of cusswords I can't repeat, and they shot down the empty hall. A bell rang and all the doors swung open. Kids rushed out, blocking our path. Uncle Spade elbowed them away, saying to me:

—You're such an idiot, Wyatt. It's almost summer and you want to start school now. What were you thinking? DANG IT! GET OUT OF MY WAY!

Everybody stared. A group of pretty girls giggled and turned their backs on us. My uncle, still talking loud, smacked open the door with the palm of his hand. I followed behind him, feeling my face burn red. As we drove away, Uncle Spade took a deep breath, lit a smoke, and grumbled at me:

—Your wrist is nearly better anyway. And you're gonna make us some money, not waste your time in a freaking place like that. We got distracted is all. We gotta get back on track, kiddo.

—I don't know what I was thinking, Uncle Spade. I'm real sorry. I guess we could cut the cast off now. The swelling's down, and besides, it's itching real bad.

So that's what we did. My uncle bought a saw at the hardware store, brought it to the parking lot, and cut the cast off. Then he returned the saw and got his money back. Lynnesha didn't say nothing about nothing, 'cause that night we left while she was at work.

CHAPTER TWENTY-TWO

I DIDN'T REALLY WANT

to go to school anyway. Seriously. My brain's just not smart that way. My brain's more fight-smart. So that's what I did: fight. One right after the next, after the next, the days starting to blur together again. And I just let it all happen, you know? When I first started traveling with my uncle, I learned quick to let the time slip by. At first, sleeping would do the trick, but after maybe eight hours, when Spade finally had to stop to sleep, all I'd do was wait. Awake and bored. So I stopped sleeping in the car and started staying still, staring. I called that Clean Time. It's the way you get after hours of the whole world whizzing past: grass and grass and trees and signs and cars and trucks and barns and fields and forests and mountains and valleys and rivers and towns and factories and bridges and cats and crows and cows and crossroads and roads crossing tracks. . . . And it all means nothing, 'cause you ain't stopping to let it in your life. Your eyes only take in shapes and colors and spaces under blue sky turning gray turning black. You don't say OOH or AAH or WOW anymore. Maybe you say:

—I wonder what that is. . . .

Your eyes stick on it, your neck swings around, holding it for just one second more before it's gone for good. But whatever it was, it's passed you by.

It's almost like dreaming without sleeping. Clean. Easy. Empties you out after so many hours. I got good at Clean Time, forgetting my achy body, my eyes and head disappearing, sounds filling them up. Especially that one sound: the road. The tires and the road, together, and that endless hum holding you till you forget you're even breathing.

After a while, I tried using Clean Time with everything Spade and me did. When I waited in the car for him to finish a deal, I'd find a close-up spot and lose myself in it. I tried to use it in diner booths while Spade told the waitress stories of things we'd never done or when he'd talk to me, driving through the desert heat, blabbing about heading to a cooler state, on and on, I'd just yawn and look out the other window.

But the problem with Clean Time is when you get good at it. Then nothing matters. You meet nice people, but you just wait for them go away and their faces fade and you don't care.

Everything stops meaning anything. I ate. I slept. I beat guys in one punch, bandaged my own hands, then took the money and left, everybody disappearing into bar darkness, cleaned away.

Let's see. . . . My second fight ever was Leland Robinson, the welder. He broke my nose for the first time. Then there was Peter Brick. He was the first guy to ever laugh right in my face. I'd smiled and tried to shake his hand, and he chuckled. Reminded me of being in school, the upper-grade kids teasing me 'cause I was so big. I didn't wanna get in trouble punching them, but I couldn't get in trouble punching Peter Brick—he lost his two front teeth on my fist for laughing. Left scars like a zipper across my right knuckles. After that, all it took was a smirk that might mean a laugh and I lost it. Like my next fight, against Mike "the Masher" Quinn, who looked down at me and smirked and I got so peeved I dumped the guy in three solids.

Next was Gordy Pace, then Big Memo Zumba, then "Keg" Oakley and then, right before Uncle Spade gave me two weeks off, there was supposed to be this kid named Curt. I don't know how he knew who I was, but he found me in the Busy Bee Diner by the train station. I was sitting at the counter waiting for my uncle to park the Chevy, when he walked right up to me, hands in his blue and gold school jacket, and said too loud:

—I'm Curt McAllister.

I smiled big as I could over my menu and said:

—I'm Wyatt Reaves, and I'm fighting you tonight.

He was just a kid. I mean, I know I was a kid too, but I was used to fighting guys, big ugly dirty ones with scars and dark eyes. This Curt McAllister kid was in high school and on the football team and known by everybody in town. He'd bring in a mound of cash, Uncle Spade explained. But I'd never beat somebody like him before, so young. Seemed wrong.

I looked him over, checking to see what I was up against. He was a good-looking guy with wide shoulders, probably real popular at school, but he stood under six foot. When I got up to shake his hand, he shoved it away and leaned up in my face.

—I'm not afraid of you.

—What?

Seeing all the people around us staring, he lowered his voice, said:

—Shut. Up.

—What's your problem? I asked.

—I'm taking you down, you big jerk.

—You can try, but I've never lost, and you're pretty small compared to me.

A man at the counter laughed. I shouldn't have said that last part, but I was telling the truth. Then the waitress came over with my coffee and stood there. Her eyes led ours to a booth full of cops in the corner. Curt took a step back, fake smiling. The fight was going to be at Buddy's, his dad's pool hall just down the street. Spade and me'd looked the place over the night before. It was bright-lit and clean for regular people to have fun, not some shack for gambling and brawls like I was getting used to.

Curt wasn't there, but Buddy McAllister gave Spade free beers and explained how his son had just started private boxing lessons. Curt wasn't too good at it and needed to know what a real fight felt like. Mr. McAllister was inviting only certain important guys to watch. Those guys'd expect a good show, so he didn't want to be disappointed. He was a big guy like me and somebody you figured you shouldn't disappoint. Him and Curt both had blond hair and blue eyes and wore dressy shirts you could tell somebody made sure had no wrinkles. Uncle Spade figured Mr. McAllister was the kind of guy who'd bet against his own son.

—How old are you? Mr. McAllister asked me.

I looked at Spade.

—He's eighteen, just like your son.

—I've won all my fights so far, I told the guy.

—Good man. I've won all my fights too, he said with a wink and chuckle.

He poured Spade another beer while they got down to money details. I picked songs off the jukebox and carved my initials in the bathroom stall before we left. I'd got in this habit every stop we made, graffitiing with a penknife my uncle had bought me. So this was what I'd do in every truck stop and diner I could: I'd find a hid spot like behind the toilet paper, then I'd cut real fast and real small, carving my initials, WR, and the month and year ('cause usually I couldn't remember the exact day) so that the next time we stopped I could see if I'd been there before. And sometimes I'd find one, like, a year later and it made me happy just knowing my life was winding around and connecting somehow, you know?

—Out. Back. Now, Curt said in a deep voice, side-looking at the cops.

—Why? I asked.

—I'm not waiting till tonight. I'm taking you on now.

—I can't. My uncle won't let me.

—Out back NOW, he said, turning to the door and elbowing people out of his way.

I didn't know what to do. If only Uncle Spade had got there right then and all those customers wasn't staring, then I could've stayed. But I didn't. I followed after him down the side alley where morning sun was cutting lines across the bricks. Curt stopped midway down, next to a old mattress leaning against the wall. He swung around with his fists up, shaking, and hollered:

—COME ON!

—I told you I can't. My uncle won't let me unless it's for money.

—I don't give a dang. I'm ready to take you down NOW, you big stupid—

I'd held back, but when he called me stupid, I moved in a step. His legs tightened. *You shouldn't tighten your legs*, Gauge Coleman taught me. *That'll be the death of you in the ring*. But I wasn't planning on socking this guy. He was breathing so quick, I thought he'd pass out soon. His blue eyes shined in the light. He looked my body up and down, trying to figure if I was getting ready to punch, but I was just standing there like a regular guy.

—You better come at me! YOU BETTER! I'M WARNING YOU!

He shook his fist, leaning too far forward. He'd lose his balance if he didn't watch it. I could've pushed him over, if I'd been close enough. His neck was thicker than mine and it jutted out of his shoulders like a tree trunk, up under his ears. He wiped sweat off his forehead and shrugged his letter jacket off. He was what Spade called a "softy," guys with calluses from gym weights and from anchoring themselves on a headboard, is what Spade said.

—Curt, I'm sorry. I ain't going to fight you now.

—Then why did you come out here? he snapped, swaying from one heel to the other.

Why *did* I go out there? To talk? Not to fight, 'cause I wouldn't break the rule. Besides, he was waiting for me to take the first swing, and I never started nothing. The other guy always had to take the first swing.

—You better defend yourself, you freak!

He came at me, first like he was unsticking his boots from mud, then like he'd tripped and was falling forward, flailing his arms around. I could've just blocked once and lifted my fist, letting his body do all the damage, but instead I swung him around in a headlock and held his arms against his chest. He squirmed. He was pretty strong, but I had him good. His back was warm and hard against me. He hollered between gritted teeth.

—Sorry, I said. I can't hit you. I told you.

—You let me go RIGHT NOW and fight!

—You already lost, I said against his ear.

—You dumb mother—

I shook him and told him to shut up. His hair caught on my wet lips. That's when I stopped smiling. I didn't know what to do with him. He wriggled against my belt buckle and tried tangling his legs in mine. I bet he was a good wrestler. He was thinking if he got me down on the ground, he could take me, sock me in the gut, knock the wind out of me. I spread my legs farther, so he couldn't get at them. The whole time he panted and grunted and wiggled, I just held him, not knowing what to do. He tried swinging his head back to clock me on the chin, but I tilted out of his way. So he yanked his arms and I squeezed his wrists till his hands, clenching and unclenching, turned purple. Partly, I liked holding him. It was safe. As soon as I let him go, even if I shoved him as far as I could, he was getting hurt. He'd get hurt either in the alley or at the bar. How'd he not know that? How'd his dad not see how easy I'd take Curt down? Now that I think about it, I guess there, behind the Busy Bee at breakfast time without a crowd, his dad wouldn't get as disappointed or embarrassed, seeing how bad his boy did. That was the safer spot. I think he was smart to end it all there.

So I hugged him in closer and rested my chin on top of his head, then closed my eyes and breathed in slow. His chest raised up and fell, slowing down. His hollering went quiet till just the two of us stood there together, tight—tighter than I ever got to another person. I could hear dishes clattering through the open kitchen door.

—Okay, I said in his ear, real soft.

And I let go and let him take the first swing. It clipped my ear, 'cause his shiny red eyes moved slower than his fist. My right foot slid back and I swung into his gut. He oofed the air out of his lungs and flopped in half.

—WYATT! Spade called from the end of the alley, but I didn't turn around. WHAT THE—?

Curt pulled himself up straight as I followed with my right, giving him one perfect, clean tap just like Gauge Coleman taught me. A flat grunt slipping out his mouth as he tipped back, his bright eyes rolling and his chin flipping up to the sky as he fell on his back. He made a tiny splash, his yellow hair mixing with the trash water. The bee-sting pain rang in my third knuckle. I grabbed it and rubbed the spot, sucking in a quick gasp like when you cry. Uncle Spade raced up and shoved my shoulder, grinding his eyebrows together.

—NEVER unless it's for money, man! THAT'S THE RULE!

I watched Curt until he wiggled like a worm and tried to open his eyes, then I started out of the alley. A couple people'd collected at the sidewalk and mumbled about the ruckus. Spade told them everything was okay, no problems, then pushed me down the street to the Chevy.

CHAPTER TWENTY-THREE

SPADE GAVE ME THEM

two weeks off he promised. But they felt more like punishment than vacation. Them two weeks turned into three that turned into a rut that turned to fall. No fairs and no fights, and I just don't think he could be bothered planning anything else. He tried, but pretty soon he was mostly sitting around at Lynnesha's, living off her and the fight money, waiting, telling me to keep up my training. I think Spade figured he should at least try to stay still awhile. Maybe for me he was trying. I don't know. But when he tried too hard for anybody but himself, things got ugly, and pretty soon a quiet built up in him, catching like a cold from him to Lynnie to me, making the house feel hollow. Spade not talking is like me not smiling: You know there's going to be trouble. More and more I was finding myself all alone, waiting, them two taking off in separate directions.

The day that quiet broke, Uncle Spade called to me from the driveway by his Chevy:

—KIDDO! COME OUT HERE!

Everything sounded dry and crisp, like the grass out in the yard that Spade refused to cut and Lynnesha wouldn't let me mow, 'cause she'd told him to do it. Grass tall enough to sway in the wind. I stepped outside, hoping Uncle Spade would be leaning on the mower handle, but instead he had two lawn chairs under one arm and his red beer cooler in the other.

—GET OVER HERE, he hollered, faking a grin. Help me with this stuff. It's heavy as a mother. Look what I got: this monster radio. Me and you are gonna put her to good use.

—Where we going? To the lake?

—You kidding me? No. We're gonna sit right here in the yard, listen to some tunes, and get plowed. Come here.

I didn't move, except to scratch the fish below my belly button. Uncle Spade could tell I wasn't sure. The chairs started slipping from under his arm.

—Dang it, Wyatt, get over here and help me, he said, his voice sounding empty.

Lately, everything he said seemed that way, on the edge of anger. I bounded over to him and took the chairs. They surprised me how light they were. I made sure I turned away from him before I said:

—Why don't we go around back—

—JEEZ-US. You scared to get some sun? No, no, no. We're staying out here.

That's when I knew he was tricking me, planning something, 'cause our family can't take much sunlight. First we get red and then more freckles. He stomped past me, lifting his feet. Then he kicked at the fall leaves, grunting and turning in a little circle till he found a flat spot, like a mutt finding its place to sleep.

—Bring them chairs, he said.

I did, and he spread them open right there in the middle of her tiny front yard, facing them into the sun, then he plopped down and patted the other seat. I eased myself down, checking to see if anybody was watching us, while he flipped through radio stations.

—I made bug juice, he said, pulling a dripping glass jug out of his cooler.

—Bug juice?

—You betcha, he said, grinning and smoothing down the edges of his mustache. It's my secret concoction, but I suppose I can share it with my only nephew. First, there's one rule you got to follow: Don't ever make it for the ladies. They can't hack it and end up puking on your shoes.

The whole thing was creeping me out. He hadn't said that much in a long time, and this playing happy was never good. He must've won the lottery or got some pot or met a new girl. I just sat there and let Spade's Mexican music fill my head.

—Listen to that sound, would you? he said, slapping his knee too fast and too hard. Here, slug some of this sucker back and feel it kick in.

He handed me the red juice. I took a small sip that burned my guts. He grabbed the jug back and downed three solid gulps.

—Know why it's called bug juice? he asked.

—Made out of bugs?

—Nah. Because, this stuff seeps out your skin and keeps the bugs away.

He laughed and passed it back to me. The booze busted up through the roof of my mouth into my brain. I wiped my mouth with the back of my hand and shuddered.

By the time Lynnesha was pulling up next to the Chevy, Spade had polished off the bug juice. I stretched my neck around to say hi, but Spade kept looking straight ahead and slapping his knee, pretending like she hadn't come home. I started to stand to help her with her groceries, but he put his hand on my shoulder and said:

—Listen to this part, man, just listen.

She got out of the car, not looking at neither of us, and

walked straight inside. That made my mouth go dry. And before the screen door even finished closing, she was rushing back out full speed. For a split second, I thought she was just going back to the car, but when the door slammed, I knew different. Uncle Spade stood up to meet her. She headed right toward him, waving her arms and spitting out words that rattled in my drunk head:

—GOD BLEEPING DANG IT, YOU SON OF A BLEEP! HOW DARE YOU SIT ON MY LAWN EMBARRASSING ME IN FRONT OF MY NEIGHBORS. I'M GONNA RIP YOUR HEAD CLEAN OFF YOUR NECK AFTER NOT ONE WORD AND NOT ONE MOMENT OF RESPECT OR DECENCY, IGNORING ME AND MAKING ME FEEL LIKE A—

She was cut off by Spade's chair slashing her across the face. He'd swung it up in one motion I could barely see, leaning forward, grabbing one chair arm and twisting it out, following the sound of her voice behind us to connect, one leg with her face, the other with her stomach, its hollow legs making a tinny noise. The chair slit her nose, but midway through the motion, he grabbed the other arm for more leverage and shoved the chair.

I get sick to my stomach picturing it again. See, the problem was: I just sat there as she stumbled back a couple of steps, arms up like maybe she could stop him, but the chair came down again, catching her across the back of the head and getting her caught in the chair frame. She flailed at him, looking like she was reaching through jail bars.

Spit shot off Spade's lips, him saying stuff I couldn't understand, but aiming it at her like she'd understood loud and clear. His knuckles went white. Finally she shook loose, but he wouldn't stop slashing and jabbing until Lynnesha caught the webbing and, with one hard jerk, pulled the chair away from him, his neck snapping forward.

—Don't. You. EVER! she screamed, throwing the chair far into the grass.

But she stopped and, keeping one sharp hand pointing at him, touched the back of her head with the other, then winced. Seeing blood stuck to her palm, she choked on her breath and screamed:

—YOU!

Uncle Spade grabbed at her, but Lynnesha shoved him with her bloody hand and he only caught her necklace in his fingers, snapping it from her neck. She set her feet solid on the ground and glared into his eyes. The chain dangled out of his raised, shaking fist.

—Go ahead, you pitiful little man. Hit me, she said, super calm and slow.

—You ain't nothing to me, my uncle told her. I got other girls.

—Big surprise, Franklin. Go ahead, hit me. I'll call the cops.

—I've been waiting to for a long time, he said, and started to swing real slow.

I leaped up and grabbed my uncle's arm, us two suddenly standing so close I looked down on him barely reaching my shoulders. His wrist felt so skinny in my fist.

—Let go, he said without breaking his stare from hers. Let go, Wyatt, right now.

Lynnesha stood there staring, not shaking like he was, just breathing fast. I didn't know what to do. Maybe if she'd looked at me just once, I'd've thrown his weak little body over her house. But she wouldn't look. Couldn't, maybe. So I let go. And he turned his back, grabbed the radio, and walked to his car. She stared into the hole in the air where Uncle Spade'd just stood.

—Lynnesha, I said. You okay?

I could see down onto her head, where the blood had matted her hair. I don't mind seeing my own blood, but seeing hers made my head swim. Spade gunned the engine, and I expected to never see him again, but he called out to me:

—WYATT, he said, NOW.

I should've stayed and taken care of Lynnesha's head, but she didn't want me. Real quick and gentle, I touched the red mark on her neck from the broke chain. She flinched and didn't turn to me, so I stepped through the high, dry grass and crumpled into the backseat.

He drove till the car was on empty and rolled it right on into a gas station. Before getting out, he noticed her charm still gripped in his fist, and, opening his fingers to let it go, I could see the metal'd made little slices in his palm. He dropped it onto the dashboard and left it there, never touching it again.

CHAPTER TWENTY-FOUR

SUDDENLY WE WERE BACK

on the road, back to fights a couple times a week. Until the Chevy broke down. We were visiting Hubcap Sandy more and more often, and the motor was getting more and more unhappy. This one time, halfway to my next fight, the thing broke down on Rural Route HH, a metal squeal coming from the engine, making me bolt straight up. Blue smoke rolled out from under the hood and turned orange in the sunset over some desert. Uncle Spade cussed and pounded his fist on the dash as he coasted to the shoulder. I was peeved too, but that smoke did look beautiful.

No cars passed, and the dry heat hurt my throat. Spade had a sweaty T-shirt wrapped around his head. He got out, cussing the road and kicking his fender. He'd planned on counting our cash that night at the New View Lodge in Toluca.

—We been there tons of times, he'd told me, stomping out his cigarette, letting the smoke leak out his nose, but I didn't remember it.

Lately we'd been feeling rich. Spade kept stuffing all the cash in a duffel bag hid under the backseat. Every night, everywheres we went, my uncle'd searched out the priciest chow in town, just 'cause he could.

My hands still throbbed from my last fight. It'd be dark soon, and I still needed to change the bloody gauze on my knuckles before I couldn't see. I climbed out of the Chevy and went to the trunk for the first-aid box. Spade still stomped around in the dust, kicking stones. As I dug in the trunk, he popped the hood to take a look, deciding he knew what was wrong. The whole car glowed red in the last few minutes of light.

—We ain't safe, he said, grabbing a bottle of whiskey off the seat and sliding down along the tire. We ain't safe with so much money and no way of protecting it.

I slid down against the other tire and tore tape with my teeth.

—We're safe, I told him.

—Kiddo, man, we got a ton of cash we got to protect.

—Spade, I'm telling you we're safe. I'll protect it.

—What we need is a gun.

—We don't need no gun, I told him, annoyed.

Man, my fists and face were throbbing. And his words was grating on my skin.

—Shut your trap, Wyatt. I'm your manager and I can get us a gun if I want.

—Manager? HA!

—Yeah, manager. I'm in charge, ain't I? Besides, I know best.

—Get me that blanket out of the trunk. I'm going back to sleep.

—You get it.

—No, you get it, MANAGER.

I'd been talking back to my uncle since he hit Lynnesha. He didn't tell me not to. I'd told him after that, after he got sober a couple weeks later, that he better not hit nobody like that again. It took me the whole week to work up to saying that and all he said was:

—I know, I know. . . .

Something started to switch then, like we were reversing our parts, me becoming the uncle, but he didn't even notice. Maybe he didn't care. Now he needed me, had to keep me fighting, earning, 'cause otherwise he'd have nothing. Finally I was worth more than just a nephew.

My head thumped with my swelling hands. I couldn't feel my fingers. I needed the blanket. Uncle Spade took a swig of whiskey and climbed up, staggering around to the back of the car. He pulled my blanket from the trunk and threw it at me, then disappeared around the other side. We stayed there all night, his snores bugging me while I laid by the bumper, using the money bag as my pillow, watching bats zigzag in the sky.

CHAPTER TWENTY-FIVE

TWO HUNTERS FOUND

Nana facedown in the woods, three pieces of glass digging into one hand.

—She'd been out collecting, Uncle Spade told me. She wouldn't stop collecting.

—How'd you find out? I asked him.

—Your dad told me.

—You talk to Fever?

—Of course I do. He's my brother.

—And he never asks to talk to me?

—And you never ask to talk to him, do you?

I didn't answer.

—We gotta go, kiddo, and we gotta hurry.

On the drive to Nana's, Spade told me everything Fever

knew, how she was in her bathrobe with the white, lacy collar, with no pajamas and no clothes, and I worried the hunters saw her naked. I squeezed that green piece of glass I'd kept and tried not to think of Nana in the clearing, two old guys smelling of booze, holding pheasants in their leather gloves and just staring at her, not wanting to touch her, 'cause her eyes were open in the grass.

—Dang, I wish you'd learned to drive, Spade said, sleepy, sipping his coffee.

—You never showed me.

—You never asked. . . .

—Well, right now's not the time, you know?

We drove straight through for near two days, Uncle Spade quiet, and me with my first-aid kit, cleaning a busted lip and keeping an ice pack on my busted ribs, thinking about maybe having to see Fever and Ma. Thinking how I wasn't going to miss Nana really, but I'd gotten used to her weird ways, you know, the heaven talk and crankiness. She was family, and like with Fever and Ma, I couldn't visit her no more. Well, actually, I did. They showed her to us in a box. In this rosy room full of rows of fold-up chairs with their backs to us. A low ceiling closed us in and a light at the front fell right on Fever by himself. He hunched over Nana laying in her plain old box. Uncle Spade moved slow to his side, but I stayed behind the rows of chairs.

The two brothers talked in mumbles with long pauses. Uncle Spade pointed to me with his chin. I kept my hands in my pockets and squeezed my piece of Nana glass. Slowly Fever turned his head. He didn't look like the guy I remembered. He used to be so big and strong and familiar. Now his dark eyes looked sunk into his head and his shoulders were hunched.

I kept his stare. I had nothing to be afraid of no more, especially being twice his size, practically. I wanted him to come stomping through the chairs, whipping them out of his way, so I could coldcock him. My feet slid back into stance, hands out, fists tightened. I felt my rib shift and sting. It's hard to believe I was expecting to fight with Nana's body laying up there. My uncle waved me closer, but I stayed put. Fever turned back to Nana, a silhouette against the cross on the wall. I punched the ceiling, leaving a dent and a booming echo in the silent building, then stomped out into the parking lot.

The sun was rising behind heavy clouds. I shook out my fists until they loosened up, then I grabbed a smoke and matches from the dashboard. Seeing Fever was excuse enough for my first cigarette, right? Besides, everybody says they calm your nerves. I held the fire to the end. It crackled and shrunk when I sucked in, the smoke jabbing the inside of my mouth and nose. Some floated into my eyes. But there was something sweet about it, not like the smoke when Fever's house burnt down. That was flat and sharp. I leaned against the Chevy's trunk, the dew wetting my butt, and closed my eyes to keep the smoke out.

I am not that weak little kid sitting in their living room, waiting for his parents to get home, I told myself. But seeing Fever suddenly made me feel tiny again in a sixteen-year-old shell. Jesus, that's what one stare could do. I opened my eyes. I couldn't breathe. My head lifted off my shoulders and bobbed up and down, my eyes not fixed on nothing. I sucked in air and, finally, a cool breeze.

Uncle Spade and Fever came out the front door, so I chucked the smoke in the wet grass where it sizzled and died, then, with my head settled back on my neck, focused on them two. I shifted into stance, but Fever didn't stop, didn't look at me. He just unlocked his car and drove off.

—Why didn't he say nothing to me?

—Give him a break, kiddo, will you? He'll talk to you soon. . . .

—Not one word, I said as we got in the Chevy.

—Christ, I know. . . . Listen, your ma ain't here 'cause of work. . . .

—I smoked one of your cigarettes, I told him.

—So? he said, pulling onto the road to Nana's. Buy the next pack.

We didn't bother turning on any lights. We ignored the whining cats, the open windows, the pee smell. Uncle Spade stayed in his old room. I slept a couple hours in the attic like normal. Fever stayed in a motel.

CHAPTER TWENTY-SIX

–YOU SHOULD CARRY THE

whole thing yourself, Uncle Spade muttered to me as we dragged the shut box out of the black station wagon.

I didn't laugh. But me carrying Nana myself would've been easier. I had to lean down, my busted ribs aching and the wood edge digging into my shoulder the whole walk to the box-shaped hole in the ground, worrying Spade'd drop her and she'd come rolling out.

At the hole, we set her down real careful. The minister squeezed his Holy Bible against his gut and some church ladies, all dressed in dark colors, sniffed into napkins. Fever dug a hole in the grass with the point of his shiny shoe. My drunk uncle closed his eyes. I should've got drunk too. And dang, my chest hurt.

We rode back to her house, not talking. The old church ladies had brought in food, their whispers burning my ears. The husbands stayed out front, waiting to leave. I stole another smoke and headed to the garbage ditch. At the bottom, away from Fever, way down by that old washer my uncle'd dragged in, I just sat on the ground and rested. And I did no crying.

On our last visit there, Nana had cornered me again. This time in the attic while I was getting dressed. She made me sit on a box, her sour mouth too close to my face, talking quick, saying:

—My sons lost Jesus and they're going to burn in hell, but you don't have to, Wyatt. Come to church. Leave them behind. Turn your life around. Are you a fornicant?

—A what? I whispered, not turning my head.

Her claw dug into my leg muscle, stinging. I wanted to give the right answer and get away, but I didn't get the question.

—No, I answered.

—Wyatt, she whispered real slow. Wyatt, love, you have to get away.

She used the word "love" and made my face turn red. I hated that word. Early that next morning, my uncle stashed more twenties around the house before we slipped out.

I shivered. The dirt was cold and the sun was gone, so I climbed out of the hole. I decided I'd go find Fever and see what he had to say to me.

He sat on the edge of a crate of glass, leaning against the living room wall, smoking and ashing into a blue bottle. His fingers were yellow from the cigarette burning down too low. The church ladies stopped, patted him on the shoulder, and said a couple nice words:

—She was a good woman . . . saintly . . . such a loss . . . so sorry . . . at peace . . .

Fever nodded at them. I nodded at them too and said thank you. They buttoned their coats and left slowly, taking their husbands from the front yard. Uncle Spade wasn't around. Just Fever and me. I wanted my dad to stand up and walk over. I wanted him to pat me on the shoulder. I wanted him to say:

—It's time to go home, son. Get your things.

And he did get up to walk into the kitchen. He passed me by, opening the fridge and leaning in, his butt sticking out like Nana's would when she eyeballed food. I ran my fingers over the plastic-wrapped plates on the table. He pulled out a beer and turned around with his eyes still on the floor, twisting off the cap.

—What? he said finally as he passed me and stopped in the doorway.

—Fever . . .

I'd worked hard on not thinking about him and Ma, but when I did, all I wanted to do was hurt them for letting me be taken away. I'd planned on burying them alive in words or hanging them off a skyscraper by their toes and watching them fall or feeding them poisoned sandwiches, but there, face-to-face with Fever, I knew he had to say something, not me. He was the dad.

—Huh, he said, like he remembered something. You don't even look like my kid no more.

He chugged his beer and turned his back; his footsteps echoed across the empty living room. The bottle crashed into the wrong colored crate and the front door slammed. He drove off, back to the City, I figured. To my ma, nothing to say.

Before we left, I done something I probably shouldn't have: I carved my initials and the date in the bathroom behind the toilet paper roll. Didn't really matter, since it wasn't nobody's house no more.

CHAPTER TWENTY-SEVEN

MY UNCLE, HE NEVER really picked the way he treated me. No matter what he tells you, he was just being himself. And Fever and Ma, they never cared enough to be good or bad. But me?

You remember my best friend, Clark? That little squirt in the trailer park I hadn't seen in two years? Every time Uncle Spade and me stayed with Edie I'd tried to hang out with him, but his mom always said Clark wasn't home or he was busy doing homework or he was at school. So I stopped trying. Well, something about that stuck with me, made me really deep-down peeved. My only friend in the world and he didn't even like me. So I got it in my head I wanted to kill him. So I blamed Clark. I was just being a idiot, I know, but I couldn't stop myself.

So when we got to Edie's this time, after Nana's funeral, I spent the first day waiting. In the same spot I used to wait. I stood in the woods, rain swirling, the sky one big cloud, watching the spot where the school bus would drop Clark off. My black curls straightened out and hung down in my eyes. Raindrops found their way between the big green leaves above me onto my face and over my eyebrows into my eyelashes, between my lips and off my chin into the mud with all the rest of the water covering the whole rest of the world. I listened to each leaf's *splat splat splat*. I could feel my muscles, too big on my bones, like knots on trees, aching from standing for so long, not moving, just staring out of the woods.

That morning, through Edie's screen door, I'd watched the trailer kids race to the bus. Two new boys Clark's size, in red baseball caps, chased him all the way up the road. Clark laughed at them. They all laughed and I watched, squeezing my Nana glass tight in one hand. Just like after a first punch in a fight, seeing Clark laugh made me kick the screen door open and run to the road. But the bus left before I could get there, its red rear lights poking through the fog by old Feegler's farm.

The rain slowed for a couple hours around lunchtime, when the mail lady waddled her route. As she passed the picnic area where Clark and me first met, she tilted the brim of her rain hat back, catching sight of me. I could've easily become a tree

176

then. My toes could've stretched down into the dirt, arms and hair and ears all sprouting leaves, green as my eyes that had turned to bark. But the mail lady lowered the flap on her hat and moved on. Drizzle slid down along the veins on my hands, collected on my pruney fingertips, and fell. I could hear Uncle Spade's hoarse voice calling out my name, letting it ping-pong off all the trailers.

That whole time waiting, I didn't think about what I was holding inside. If I'd known it was cool meanness I had in me, cool meanness like Spade's got, maybe I would have walked away. It wasn't the mad I got from fighting, but a metal taste slick in my mouth.

When the bus stopped and sighed its door open, I sucked in the biggest breath my lungs would take and balled up my fists, squishing the water out. Clark hopped out of the bus from the top step by the driver. A bunch of kids piled out after him, most taking off fast as the bus pulled away. But those two red-capped boys stayed behind. I took a step, my knee cracking. Then I lifted my arms to spread the branches around my head and stepped out of the woods.

All three of them stomped in the puddles leading into the park. As they reached the UNCLE SAM'S sign, only a couple of trailer-lengths away from me, I could hear them.

—You idiot. You're going to get my homework soaked, Clark said.

—No duh, said one boy.

—Like that would suck, said the other.

Both red-capped boys stomped again, making Clark turn his back against water and catch sight of me standing in the spot where I'd always waited for him. The other boys followed his eyes and froze in their puddles, seeing a tree trunk take a step. My knotty arm muscles shifted, swung with my legs, my skin crackling like a tree struck by lightning. The soles of my sneakers squished the grass past the picnic bench. The Red Caps wiped rain from their eyes.

—Who is that, Clark?

—Is that . . . ?

—The freak kid from the pink trailer?

—What's he doing?

—Is he coming over here?

—He's coming for you, Clark.

—Doesn't look too happy . . .

My body chopped through the misty drizzle between us, my eyes locked with his. Clark had turned into a turtle, his big knapsack hunched over his scrawny shoulders, head lowered, trying to tuck it away from me. The Red Caps backed up, telling Clark to run. Those stupid boys disappeared, leaving Clark on the edge of the road just a couple paces away from me and my fists. Gosh, that electricity running through my muscles, itching the skin on my skull, it sent a message into my brain, blaming this little kid for everything. It blamed him for ditching me, for picking those two darned Red Caps over me, for Spade, for Fever walking away, Lynnesha and Nana gone, for none of life being right.

—Wyatt? he asked as he stepped back, ankles wobbly.

I stepped onto the road and stopped.

—Hi, he said, his voice sounding so regular.

I expected him to sound jumpy, maybe say something different.

—Shut up, I said, and grabbed him by the neck.

—WYATT REAVES, Uncle Spade called, stretching it out like a exhale of smoke.

I looked toward the shout, feeling Clark's eyes sticking on me.

—What happened to you, Wyatt? Where'd you go? Man oh man, you got gigantic.

I squeezed his throat before I could even look back at him, my whole hand wrapped around his puny neck. He gagged and gurgled. I needed to talk. I wanted words to tell him, but nothing came out my mouth.

—I thought we were—

—YOU LITTLE—SHRIMP—RAT—DUMB—, I spit between my teeth, STUPID—MEAN—I hate you. I knocked and I waited and I thought I'd go to school and protect you and you didn't answer. You leave me like Fever—

—Fever? he squeezed out before I could tighten my grip again.

I didn't have no more words to say, so I shook him.

—I'm sorry, he wheezed, his tiny hands trying to wrap around my wrist. Please don't kill me.

Wind whipped us frantically, and I let go. I maybe cried then. I couldn't tell. I can't tell now. With rain streaming down my face, it got hard to breathe, like squeezing my own throat.

—I want it all back, I choked out.

—What? He rubbed the red marks on his throat.

—YOU'RE A LIAR, CLARK KENT, I growled.

—What? he repeated. WHAT?

A Red Cap popped around the corner of a blue trailer and disappeared again. Moms started showing up. I had to decide what to do.

—What, Wyatt?

He didn't understand nothing, couldn't see out of his normal life into mine. And I couldn't explain it. He took two steps back, his eyes darting to where the Red Cap boys hid.

—You're just a kid, I said. You wouldn't understand.

—You're just a kid too.

—NO! YOU ARE JUST A STUPID LITTLE KID!

My fists tightened.

—CLARK! RUN, MAN! hollered a Red Cap, still hid.

—Well, you're just a stupid BIG kid, Clark said.

—No, I'm not. I'm not no kid no more.

I realized one punch and he'd be in the hospital for a month, so I let my fists drop.

—What's the big deal, Wyatt? We were friends. Now we're not. So what? he said.

And I shoved him down. A grunt of air pushed out of him. His glasses shot off. The back of his head knocked the road and bounced, his knapsack holding him up like a pillow.

—Hey there, kiddo, Spade said soft, touching my arm. Why don't you let the shrimp go?

The flag stopped flapping. Edie held the Red Caps' shoulders. A group of moms under umbrellas collected behind her, behind the UNCLE SAM'S sign, safe from the humongous wacko picking on the little boy.

—He ain't worth it, Spade said, and waved Clark away.

All in one motion Clark hopped to his feet, scooping up his beer-bottle glasses and scrambling toward the others. I shook loose from Spade's touch and breathed in the fear that hung around me. Even Spade was wondering what I'd do next, and I could've done anything I wanted. I was hardwood walking, and I marched straight through the frightened crowd, shaking my head to splatter water over them as I said:

—Spade, we're getting out of this stupid place.

Once I'd passed the women, they started talking about me, and about Clark, asking was he okay. Back at Edie's trailer, I grabbed our bags off the floor and pitched them into the Chevy. Spade jogged up and stopped by the driver's side, huffing, his hands shaking.

—We just got here, Wyatt, and I ain't—

—Spade, we're out of here, I said, slamming the back door.

He opened his mouth to put me in my place, but I looked into him and he saw me, saw the big peeved guy clenching his jaw. I stood ready for anything, and then, like I'd focused my whole body on it, the sun spurted out of the clouds and over the car, lighting up the last raindrops. He closed his mouth, and by midnight we were at the Lucky Rabbit Motel, same room as the night before, me staying real quiet just like Spade.

CHAPTER TWENTY-EIGHT

LIKE ME, RAMON CAIDA,

"The Mexican Maniac of Montusa," hadn't never lost a fight, but he was old (like thirty maybe, or older), so I wasn't worried.

—I can take him in four, I told Spade.

—You haven't even seen the guy fight, my uncle grumbled, dumping sugar in his cup.

—I don't need to, I said, handing the waitress my menu. Gimme the special, I told her.

—Huh, Spade said. Gimme that special too.

—You against me? I asked him.

—Course not. But you gotta stay focused, keep working out.

—I AIN'T going on a beer run, if that's what you're getting at.

—I ain't saying that. I'm saying you gotta do SOMETHING.

—I'll do SOMETHING. I'll take him down.

I told him every day how I was going to beat Ramon Caida and he better back me, but I didn't work out the day of the fight or the day before, just 'cause Spade kept telling me to.

I'll never forget that nasty joint. No name on the place. Just a neon cactus hanging under a awning that covered plastic tables and chairs. The dirt yard was surrounded by a high wall topped in broke glass. So much dancing, so many fighting feet had made the ground hard as bricks, smooth like linoleum. Must have been forty guys all shuffling their boots, waiting, while ladies in white cutoff T-shirts served free tequila shots. These guys had paid to get in. Señor Cortina, the bar owner, collected bets and talked up Ramon. All eyes glanced off me sitting in the corner taping up and smirking at them like a idiot.

Ramon Caida swaggered through the crowd wearing a red silk bathrobe just like real boxers do, and he tore it off a minute before the fight started. Everybody patted him, said nice stuff in Mexican. He didn't stretch, so neither did I. Señor Cortina called me up to the front and explained how important this fight was. He said some stuff I didn't understand, then in English he said he couldn't take no more bets. That got boos. I looked Caida up and down, his shaved head and thick shoulders, and his eyes and feet that never stopped moving. His skin was so dark you could barely tell he had snake tattoos up each arm. I pulled my shorts down just enough so you could see the teeth on my tattoo.

His first punch got me going, but it surprised me, so solid and quick. He kept his eyes on mine, never flinching, not even when I knocked out two of his side teeth. They cut up the white tape and the back of my hand. He just spit the bloody teeth out and kept dancing. I wiped my slashed skin on my shorts and felt the burn. By this time, after fighting for years, I was barely noticing pain. I just put the cuts and scrapes in Clean Time. It all goes away sooner or later.

Ramon Caida turned up the energy, like I counted on. All I needed to do was block till he got tired. But he was quick and I caught one in the jaw. I saw sparks and had to shake them off, backing up a second. Searching the edge of the loud crowd, I found my uncle's face, wrinkled up, worried. That made my belly flutter. I stepped back in. We circled. I doubled down— block, jab, jab. And I missed. He moved quicker than me. His right hook snuck up, clobbering my eye so hard it felt sunk into my brain. My open eye saw his left catch my mouth and crack this front tooth out, a gurgling blood noise sneaking out of me as I went down. The crowd clapped, leaning in. Señor Cortina shoved them back. The lights got brighter, filling my eyes as I climbed up, spitting. I tried to get it together, but he followed me. I circled, ducked, and blocked; he was there, close in, his fists in my belly. When the final blow came at my head, I didn't see it. I could hear the shouts and cheers and cusswords, and the thud of my own body slamming that hard dirt. It smelled like liquor. They turned off the lights. Everybody went quiet. My body disappeared. The radio lost its signal and the static buzzed.

My uncle and a doctor propped me on a chair in the dirt yard. They stared. The doctor patted my shoulder. He'd already cleaned up the gash on my hand from Caida's teeth.

—I ain't fighting no more, I tried spitting through my swelled lips.

—What? they asked.

My face was so puffed up and hurt so bad I had to work at saying:

—NO MO FITS.

—Yeah, yeah, Spade said, shaking his head. No more fighting. Right. Now shut up, while he stitches up your eyebrow.

We were the only ones out there. Wind flapped the awning. The cactus was turned off. Spade didn't wave no wads of money in my face like usual, and instead tossed back another tequila shot. I closed my eye and felt the needle break my skin, then poke and poke and poke.

CHAPTER TWENTY-NINE

AFTER ME ALMOST KILL-ing Clark, and the Chevy always falling apart and me not fighting since Caida, we didn't really got nowheres else to go and nothing to do. My uncle and me had made our life suck so much we was stuck there in Montusa. Uncle Spade gave up on moving around and settled us into room 16B, all the way at the far end of the Sunset Motel, away from the office, so he could do a different kind of selling. He tried to keep it from me, but I knew he always had to be selling something. He slept late every day, not going out, and he didn't even have a ladyfriend in town. That's how bad it was. When Uncle Spade did take me driving for supplies or a meeting, the Chevy grumbling along, I couldn't sit still. I'd jiggle my legs, scoot down in the seat, roll the windows up and down, tap the dash to a tune. He worked hard at not saying nothing to me, grumbling to himself like a homeless guy, until he couldn't take it no more and shouted:

—WYATT, STOP THAT!

We were staying too long. Just like him, I'd got used to the road humming under me. I told him I needed to move, but he didn't listen, so I'd take off on my own. Soon as I woke up, I went walking. Sometimes I headed straight into the woods across the road. Other times, I'd go into town and out the other side till I reached the highway and couldn't go no farther without hitchhiking (which, believe me, I thought about lots of times, standing on the shoulder, cars whizzing by). The people in Montusa must have thought I was some loony wandering around every day.

I liked the place. The downtown was built up a hill that started at this bridge over a gully with a stream where fishermen lined up in rubber pants. The downtown had maybe fifteen shops, and half of them was bars. All of them looking like a fake cowboy town. At the top of the hill, just as you hit the curve, a bunch of church towers stuck up above the houses on tiny streets with no sidewalks, so people walked and biked and drove in the road. In the City you'd never walk in the street, unless a stranger was following you home from school. Pretty soon I stopped walking by their houses, 'cause I figured people'd call their one cop on me. Instead I stopped into the churches. They left them unlocked all night. Can you believe that? I could have stole any of those Jesuses and candles I wanted, but I didn't. I just wandered around, looking at the pictures and colored-glass windows until a priest guy tried talking to me. Then I moved on. Pretty soon I ran out of churches, so I passed them, past Montusa High School, to Coal Pete's Grocery, where I could buy pops and chips and sit out front where nobody bothered me. I bought myself other junk too, 'cause I had my own money to spend, like deodorant and a shaving kit and a real cool hairbrush. Problem was, no matter what I did, I felt trapped, going crazy.

CHAPTER THIRTY

THIS ONE NIGHT, I WENT
to cool off at the motel pool. I grabbed that *Book of Mormon* from the bedstand and a towel, then threw them on a chair by the lit-up water. I can't swim, so I kicked big splashes in the shallow end till my fingers puckered up like raisins, then I let my body float, keeping my arms resting on the edge. I'd dried off and was trying to read that weird book about battles and vineyards when I saw Spade prop open the door, the radio cranked. I guess he must've finished his business and was having a beer with his visitor. I was watching the blue light from the water make the pages look rippled, when I heard Spade holler.

A short guy darted out our motel room and huffed it across the parking lot, weaving between the cars, going full swing. You could tell he was drunk or maybe on something, 'cause his legs stumbled out from under him a little. It was so quiet I could hear his breathing over the crunch of the gravel. Spade appeared in the doorway, one hand cupping his left eye. He waved a gun, a trickle of red running down his cheek.

—GET HIM! he yelled. WYATT, GET THAT KID!

Seeing the gun and Spade's blood made my skin sizzle like when I fought. I jumped up, my towel slipping into the blue water, and hopped the low chain-link fence into the parking lot, chasing after him, barefoot. I shouted, STOP, but the guy didn't slow down. He ducked around a old brown station wagon. I ran all out, my arms chugging at my sides. Just before the corner by the motel office, I caught him, my hands fumbling for the collar of his sweaty T-shirt. I yanked him backward by the shirt, gagging him. His ankles slid out from under him and he dropped, feet slipping between mine and tangling me up, making me fall after him, raising dust. I wasn't expecting that at all, so I went down heavy, my hip bone smacking his rib cage, my elbow clipping his cheek. He grunted, then moaned. The only thing I could do to control him was find his wrists and grab them. Then I flipped him onto his back and pinned him down. His chest heaved under a shirt that said LEGALIZE on a big palm leaf and smelled like beer and sweat.

—Don't hurt me, mister, he said, looking up at me through glassy blue eyes. He had high cheekbones that made him look like a girl.

—GOSH, I said, throwing my leg over him and straddling his belly. I told you to stop.

—Mister, I didn't do nothing, MISTER, honest to God.

—Honest to God? I asked, 'cause it sounded weird to me. What'd you do to my uncle?

—Your UNCLE?

—You hurt him and he's bleeding, you little jerk.

—Come on. I didn't do nothing. Let me go, he said, his pimply face flinching.

—No.

—Please, he said, wriggling his wrists and twisting his stomach under my body.

—No.

—Spade, he fell, man. FELL. I was getting another beer, and he was shouting at the weatherman or something and he just stumbled. Hit his head on the TV. I SWEAR.

—Get up, I said, keeping a hold on him as I sprang to my feet, gravel stuck in my knees.

—BRING THAT MAGGOT OVER HERE, Spade called out over the cars.

—What'd you do? I asked, jerking him up.

He wrenched his wrists free and rubbed their red spots. The hair on top of his head was all greasy and dusty and sticking up.

—I said, what'd you do?

—Nothing, he blurted, getting a little peeved now that he was out from under me.

—WYATT? Spade said, sounding overtired, maybe weak from losing blood.

I put my hand on the back of this guy's neck and called to Spade:

—I GOT HIM.

The motel lights and pool blue mixed together on us, making this all seem fake. And I didn't like the way this whole thing felt. The guy kept his head down. It was like the two of them didn't know what to say to each other. I let go of his neck. Spade leaned on the door, his fist against his mouth, the gun hanging loose in his other hand. The radio chattered behind him. Spade'd smeared the blood across his cheek, where it'd dried dark like the bags under his shiny eyes.

—What'd he do, Uncle Spade?

—Where's the stuff, Phil? Spade said into his fist.

—I don't got it, Spade Man.

—What stuff? I asked.

—Bull. You took it and ran.

—I did not! You were freaking me out and I ran.

—BULL. Show me your pockets, Spade said, waving the gun in the guy's face.

—No, Spade, I said. Put the gun away.

—It was on the bed, Spade, I swear.

—Yeah, it was on the bed and you took it.

Spade slapped his palm against Phil's chest, which Phil shoved away, saying:

—Look for it. It's there. We had a deal, man. I don't pull stuff like that.

I pushed past Phil to go look and settle this whole thing before somebody called the cops, but Spade blocked me.

—I'll check, he said. You watch this little freak.

Spade turned and wobbled, but steadied himself before he walked over between the beds, kicking empty cans out of his way. His eyes shifted around, then stopped. He dropped to his knees and stretched an arm under the crumpled bedspread. There was a crinkling noise as he fumbled around. Spade sat up holding a little clear Baggie of pot, which he stuffed in his pants pocket. It looked too tiny to fight over.

—Let him go, Wyatt. I got it. But tell him to never come back here.

—You're crazy, Spade, Phil said. You stay away from me.

Phil looked up at me, mouth twitching, and repeated himself before he took off running. I watched until he disappeared past the office. The water faucet hissed. There was some rustling, then Spade came back into the room, patting his face with a towel, and dropped into the chair. He wasn't holding the gun. He'd hid it behind the toilet, I think. The cut above his eyebrow was a tiny nick, but it sure had bled a lot. He cracked open another beer. I couldn't take his junk no more. I lit one of his smokes.

—Spade, look at me.

He didn't look at me.

—Look at me. I'm serious.

—Go to bed, kiddo.

—Listen to me, I said slow, and took a drag. I'm trying to tell you something.

—Shut up.

—No, you shut up.

—Are you talking back to me?

—Just listen.

—You do what I tell you.

—But—

—Go to bed.

—But getting me into stuff like this, I said, pounding the doorjamb.

—This was nothing, kiddo. Just a misunderstanding. Won't happen again. No more gun, okay? Everything's fine. Let me drink in peace, will you?

I stood there, trying to think what to do. There had to be something. I stabbed out the smoke. The book and towel were still outside, so I crossed the parking lot, the gravel biting my feet. Bending down for the book, I noticed little pieces of gravel still stuck to my knees. I picked them out of the dents they'd made. Then I knelt by the water to scoop out the towel, but it'd floated too far toward the deep end. I couldn't go in there. I was just a dumb guy who couldn't swim. What could I do? Man, I got so peeved. I couldn't figure what to do, so I chucked that stupid book into the trees. It tore through the leaves and landed heavy. I hoped I got in trouble, hoped the motel charged Spade a million bucks.

The room door still stood open, Spade sitting in the dark, loads of cans around him. I stopped in the doorway. When his eyes finally caught on me filling the frame, I said:

—Spade, I want to go back . . . to Fever and—

—Go. Get out of here. I don't need you, he mumbled, swinging his loose hands like smoke got in his eyes, his beer sloshing. I mean it: I don't need you around anymore.

—Shut up, I said real quiet, looking at a big wet spill on the carpet.

—I don't need you, he said again. And you don't need me. Nobody needs nobody. Your dad thought he needed me. Wrong. Lynnesha, she thought the same. Wrong, wrong, wrong. None of them need me. Just think they do. Like your ma needing your dad. Like you—you don't need me for nothing . . . except a car ride, he said with a chuckle, then choked on a sip of beer.

I looked at him real good: his skin like a greasy diner, his black eyes like spiders in holes, his body like a starved bird. He was a stranger. We spent every day together and I never knew what he was thinking, him never telling me nothing he didn't have to.

—So why'd you keep me around so long, then? I asked him, feeling shrunk back to twelve and a half. Why'd you do that?

Even before the answer, I felt better. Without knowing it, I'd been holding that in like a breath under water. His eyes drooped a little, then snapped open and found me.

—Huh, he said. Huh, yeah. You're right. Why you been around so long? I mean, I kept you with me as a favor to your dad. And you were so quiet, like a puppy. I mean you didn't have nowheres to go. What was I going to do, leave you with Lynnesha?

—Yeah, you could've left me with Lynnesha, sure, or taken me back to Fever, but you kept me around, 'cause you needed me. Didn't you?

—What? No. You're a silly, silly, silly kid. Silly, silly. He took a gulp and shook his head. You don't get it, do you? You earned me money—

—Yeah, but before that. And now. What about that? And why get me a tattoo? Why buy me stuff and tell me I done good? Why—?

—Shoot. Life just ain't that simple. I kept you around minute to minute, man. There was plenty of times I thought I'd just pull away without you, walk out and leave you with the bill.

—But you didn't. . . .

—You're just my puppy. He busted out laughing, Here, boy. Heel, Rover.

—Shut up, I said.

—Fetch, kiddo! he said, tossing his beer can at me.

—YOU'RE THE KID, I shouted, stomping off.

I jumped into the deep end, not even plugging my nose, held the side, and grabbed my towel out. Then I stayed there by the pool, thinking hard as I could and shivering, until the sun started coming up.

CHAPTER THIRTY-ONE

CAN YOU SEE YOURSELF?

I can't. I try. I've tried lots of times. And that morning I tried too. At dawn I headed back. The room door still stood open, Spade still slumped in the chair. I left him there and stood in front of the whole-body mirror on the back of the bathroom door. I stripped down (even my underwear), and still I couldn't see who everybody else said I was. I didn't see none of them things: the beast, the freak, the puppy, the giant, tough as nails, and so serious, so quick to fight. Looking in my own eyes, I saw the same as always: that kid who took one last shower in his folks' house just before he burnt the place down. Looking down, I saw the guy with the big veins running down hard arms and the thick blue lines of the nightmare fish, his tattoo teeth still sharp, ready to attack. I scratched the hair down there. I held my parts in both hands. I smiled and stuck my tongue in the hole of my missing tooth. My own face, it changed every time I looked at it: Evil. Lost. Happy. Ugly. Tan. Beautiful. Pale. Crooked. Just right. I growled. I yelled. I dragged my fingers down my cheeks, leaving red marks. Which one is me? Am I mean? Am I good? Am I good-looking? I turned to the sink and filled it with hot water. Then I shaved with the razor and foam I'd bought at Coal Pete's. Got rid of those skinny hairs under my nose. No matter how careful I was, it hurt like crazy. Cut myself twice, too. But that change was worth it.

CHAPTER THIRTY-TWO

I SHOOK SPADE'S NAKED
arm hard as I could. He waved his hand like he was swatting at flies. I shook him again and hollered in his ear:

—GET UP!

He looked up like he'd never seen me before and wrapped his pasty arms around his chest. I yanked him out of the chair and handed him his pants. Our bags was already packed into the warming-up Chevy, exhaust blowing in the open door. Spade stumbled trying to get into his pants, so I held him up. He started to ask questions, but the words mushed on his lips. I lit a smoke and passed it to him. He stood still a second, holding up his pants, looking into my face.

—It's too dang early, he growled, and took a drag.

—Spade, it's past noon.

—Where we going?

—The City. You're taking me to Ma and Fever.

—What? Why?

—Because, I said, pulling the cigarette from his fingers and handing him a clean T-shirt.

Smoke drifted out of his cracked lips. He didn't ask about the loot under the bed. I'd split up the cash, stuffed it in two garbage bags, and tossed his half in the trunk with his stash. And I'd hucked his gun into the woods. I checked: It was empty. After he smashed out the last of his smoke, he started to say something, but I handed him his sunglasses and walked him out by the shoulder. The only thing I left in that smelly room was a giganto tip with a note:

Thanks, maids. You were real nice.

—Wyatt Reaves

Spade dropped in behind the wheel and I got in next to him. He lowered his glasses down his nose, eyeing the clean seats. No more junk food bags or beer cans or mud. Nothing. The dashboard shined—even Lynnesha's charm that'd melted into the vinyl. I handed him a foam cup of coffee and told him to drink, then took it back and lit one more smoke before he pulled out, the tires kicking gravel at the door to room 16B.

We drove all day, not saying nothing. I wasn't too sure if

he remembered us talking the night before, but I did, and I didn't have no more to say. At sunset I saw skyscrapers poking the air above the highway, all lit up and warning me. Just as the buildings started to close in around us, Spade pulled off the expressway and wound through familiar streets. Without even looking, he drove me past the empty lot where the house used to be, stopping only three blocks down, in front of a little brick apartment building. He hung over the steering wheel, his eyes like cigarette burns in a white sheet. I knew he was in pain after driving all day—hungry, thirsty, confused—but I couldn't care. I climbed out and grabbed my bags from the backseat.

—Thanks, Uncle Spade . . . for the ride.

Apartment 3 said REAVES. I stood on the step, looking at the sun falling between the buildings and listening to the Chevy rattle down the street.

CHAPTER THIRTY-THREE

I GUESS I NEVER REALLY

said why I took off with Uncle Spade. I don't even like thinking about it, but I remember it was a Saturday, and it was a lot
of years ago on my twelve-and-a-half birthday, and it'd been
six days without me seeing my folks. I mean, maybe they did
come home when I was sleeping or at school, but I got ready
for my first day of seventh grade by myself, and I made soup
every night and did homework and got ready for bed by myself.
I might've been just the tallest, scrawniest kid around, still too
scared to do anything I shouldn't, but on that Saturday I woke
up thinking, *This is my half birthday, and today my folks are
gonna come home for me.*

—HELLO, I called out. HELLO HELLO HELLO . . .

Man, I hated the quiet in that old house. I made my feet

smack against the hardwood floor and flicked the padlock holding shut Ma and Fever's room as I passed by (he'd put it there to keep me from poking around). See, usually there'd be noise all night when I tried to sleep. My ma'd shatter beer bottles against the wall and blare the TV or Fever'd drink bourbon out of the bottle and play solitaire sprawled across his bed, screaming about how the cards was cheating him. So that quiet meant my folks were maybe at a job, or a second job, or a third. My ma always worked as a temp and Fever usually had car jobs: washing them, gassing them, or selling car radios with some guy called Sticky Mickey. Their work shifts changed so much I couldn't keep up. And when they weren't at a job, they were out there in the City somewhere, Ma with her gals and Fever with his pals, down at the shops or up at the bar or sitting on stoops or cruising around.

I grabbed a can of pop from the fridge and a bag of nachos off the counter, turned on the TV in the living room, and cranked up the volume. I swigged soda pop and thought about leaving. I wanted to walk right out the door and never see that peeled paint or rotted wood ever again.

Fever and Ma, they hated that house too. Granny left it to Ma after she croaked. See, Ma was sixteen when I was born. Fever, he wasn't much older, but still dumb enough to marry her, he'll tell you. He'd just moved to the City with his little brother, Spade, to find work. He stopped Ma on her way to school and told her all the stuff girls like to hear. That's the way the story goes, anyway. Two years later Granny died, leaving her sour ghost behind in that stinky house off the expressway. I guess that's why my folks stayed away as best they could.

—Maybe I'll go outside, I said out loud. Maybe go play, you know. Find some friends. And maybe I just won't come back.

I started make-believing where I'd go:

—Edgeville and Springfield and Crestwell . . . , listing all the places I'd heard of, . . . Arizona and Pittsburgh . . . and Edgeville and . . .

I didn't know very many places back then. Somewhere there had to be a book that'd show everywhere in the world I could go. I flipped through my schoolbooks but couldn't find a map. Maybe Fever had one. He kept a couple books hid in their room.

I spun the combination I'd seen him do, slid the lock off, and dropped it on the floor. Swinging the door open, I yelled just to make noise:

—MA, YOU THERE? FEVER?

The air stunk like work boots and mildew, since they didn't trust the Leoni boys next door and never opened their window. I crouched next to the bed, swiping dust bunnies out of the way, and found some ragged newspapers, one dusty black high-heeled shoe, a little silver can, and a pile of books. I brushed all of the extra junk out of the way and looked at the stack: *1989 Complete Guide to Hot Rods*, *1001 Secrets to Starting Your Own Small Business*, *Holy Bible*, and *The Joy of S-E-X*. I didn't figure the Bible had any maps, so I shoved everything back under except the newspaper comics and held up the little silver can. It was a Sterno. One winter when the gas got cut, my folks used them for cooking. I took it, tucked the comics under one arm, and locked the door behind me.

In the living room, with the blinds shut and the television blaring, "You're the next contestant on *The Price Is Right*," I sat on the floor to take off my sneakers and crossed my legs so I could read. Most of the time I didn't care about the smell of beer spills and cigarettes, but mixed with the stink from my one pair of jeans I could barely stand it, so I breathed through my mouth.

I sat between Ma's couch and Fever's recliner—never on their furniture. They got peeved with me real easy. They were always shutting me up with shouts and waves. Said they were always tired, annoyed, and didn't have time. So I'd make sure there was nothing for me to knock over and always emptied their overflowing ashtrays.

Once, Fever came home to find me playing cars with Scotty Rogers, my one school friend, and started hollering:

—DANG IT, kid, what are you doing? Who the heck is this?

Only he didn't say "dang" or "heck."

—Scotty, I said. He's in my class. We asked his dad if he could come over and—

Fever cut me off, talking real low and quiet, explaining:

—So I come into my own house to find you two here alone, getting into trouble, and what? Cutting each other's heads off with a butcher's knife, and then what? I'd be headed for jail. You see where I am going with this? Listen, Scotty, go on home now. . . . And you, you little runt, to your room. Do some homework or something. Go on—NOW!

And after that Scotty Rogers wouldn't come over no more.

I flapped the comics open hard as I could. When I smoothed the pages down, I noticed my fingernails were dirty. That bugged me. Dirty nails was just a regular, everyday thing, and this was my half-birthday party. I popped the top off the Sterno. Inside was this thick jelly stuff like volcano lava. It was the orange color of pumpkins and when I lit it, the can glowed like a jack-o'-lantern. It was like having a mini-fireplace. And now it felt more like a party.

The first comic was always *Peanuts*. I pointed at each box with one finger and mouthed the words slowly. I mostly got the idea from the pictures of Snoopy and Linus and Charlie Brown. It was a good one. The kite-eating tree was always hilarious. I laughed out loud. It felt good, sounded good. So I laughed louder, forcing it up from my guts, making my chest and shoulders shake, like I was a cartoon character. HA HA HAAA! I pushed it out of my body as hard as I could. Maybe it could break all the windows and explode into the neighbors' houses so they'd wonder who was having so much fun.

Is that kid next door having a party with lots of people and friends? they'd say. *Why weren't we invited?*

I heaved the laughs harder until I had a headache. Turning the page, I followed Dagwood out the door on his way to work, knocking the postman over, envelopes everywhere. HA HA HA! I tilted my head back, throwing the laughs out the front window, along the street, where they'd burst in my folks' ears like a sudden gust of wind wherever they were. They'd reach Ma, and she'd look up, blinking her eyes, her oversize earrings jingling, and say:

—Golly, gals, I gotta get home to my son, make him some supper, play some Scrabble.

Or they'd find Fever leaning forward on his bar stool, cocking his head, stubbing out his smoke, saying:

—Shoot, guys, I gotta get home, make sure my son's okay, make sure he's happy, laugh with him maybe.

But after I finished reading even the soap opera comics, still no one came home. And I stopped laughing. My party was over, all the chips and pop gone. I sat cross-legged in the shadowy house in the middle of the dirty living room, stinky and alone, not knowing if anybody would come home ever again, and I tore the comics into long strips.

The first one burnt quick. The fire licked the paper until it got too close to my fingers; then I let go and the blackened paper floated like magic to the ceiling. I picked up another and burnt it, watching it float. The flakes of ash were like crows, I thought, flying around my head. Some of them still burned and settled on the brown rug, on Ma's couch, on Fever's recliner. One wouldn't float. It burnt my fingers and I tossed it away, onto the curtains, a sizzling hole appearing like a stain.

I didn't care about those gross curtains. I didn't care about nothing. I kept lighting the comic strips on fire and let those curtains keep burning. A flame jumped out of the carpet, but I lit another one and watched it lift into the air. Butterflies. That's what they were, black butterflies. They'd fly and land, flutter and float. Some spun in loops near the ceiling and into the kitchen. Smoke swooped into the dark hallway, and my seeing got fuzzy.

I lifted into the air, my eyes leaving my body on the floor. I was floating. Swooping. Finding the draft. Finding a crack under the door to flutter out of the house above the rows of gray houses and their tiny brown lawns, over the cracked street covered in trash and broken glass, way way over the express-way. Toward the clouds. That's where I'd go. To the clouds. But I started hacking and plunged back into my body.

My belly shook from coughing. The smell wasn't just paper burning now, but plastic and wood. My head spun. I squeezed my eyes shut, then puked chips and pop on the leftover comics, my throat and mouth sizzling. Flames burst from the couch. I yanked my arm away, jumped up, and scrambled to the front door.

The three deadbolt locks fought the wood. Heat ran up my back. As the door came open and I lurched down the front steps, my brain turned up my hearing—fire crackling, TV blaring inside, little kids on roller skates down the block, neighbor's radio blasting, and shouts:

—OH GOD, OH GOD, Mrs. Leoni shouted, her slippers slapping down the sidewalk to where I watched the smoke puff out the door. WYATT! What's happening? Oh fire! Oh FIRE!

More neighbors flooded out their doors, but I couldn't look at any of them. I just watched the flames. Strangers bumped against me, filling the street and blocking traffic. Mr. Leoni tried to stretch his garden hose over the fence, but it wouldn't reach. I heard sirens howl and come closer.

—Where are your folks, Wyatt?

—What happened? Who did this?

—OH, MAN, COOL! Will you look at that!

—Get the boy a blanket. He's barefoot, for God's sake.

—Mary, Jesus, and Joseph. Please Lord help us.

—Ay, por Santo Dios . . .

A blanket fell over my shoulders, and somebody helped me across the street to where I couldn't feel the heat no more. Fire guys popped open the hydrant at the corner and dragged the thick canvas hose to the flames. The first jet of water shot in the front door, hissing, sending more thick smoke out. It took two guys to hold the hose. The whole house snapped and cracked. Ambulances showed, and cops. News crews and a long black station wagon like the one Nana got put in. People passing patted me on the shoulders and hung their heads. I stayed mixed in with the crowd, my head sticking up above most everybody.

My folks didn't show up until the roof'd started to cave in. Fever ran up full speed, his unbuttoned shirt flapping. A cop held him back, but Fever yanked away, his head darting around. Then he pounded on the blue hood of a cop car, over and over. Ma hopped off the expressway bus through a cloud of smoke. Coughing, she pushed past the crowd, yanking at her hair and hollering as loud as the sirens:

—THAT'S MY HOUSE! THAT'S MY HOUSE!

I just stayed where I was, hid behind the other faces, covering my smile with the blanket, watching my folks finally get home and those thousands of ash butterflies fluttering into the air toward the clouds.

By the next morning, I'd be putting that whole mess out of my head, pretending it never happened. I'd be sneaking out of the City Shelter, shoeless, following my cool uncle into his gigantic, shiny white car and speeding away from the smoking hole in the ground I'd just made, a big smile on my face.

CHAPTER THIRTY-FOUR

THE BUILDING DOOR WAS open, so I climbed the stairs up to Apartment 3 and knocked. It took a minute before Ma opened the door, and looking up at a oversize guy with a missing-tooth grin, she asked me if there was a problem. It'd been five years. She looked older and angrier, with big dark bags under her eyes. I froze, and she started closing the door until I squeezed out:

—Ma?

She looked up into my face, then shook her head, not smiling or nothing. Instead she just waved me in, and I followed her down a skinny hall into a mini-kitchen.

—What are you doing here?

—I just come to see you two. That's all.

—Your dad worked a double shift, she explained, but he'll be home soon. Want coffee?

—Coffee? Yeah. Uh, yes, please.

—Sit, she told me.

—I . . .

—Sugar? Cream? We only got milk.

—Drink it black, I told her.

—Where's your uncle?

—On the road, I said.

—Are you staying awhile?

I shrugged and nodded.

—We got a junk room you can use while you're here. Just clean it out and get a bed.

—I don't sleep in a bed, Ma.

—I'll put your bags in there for you, she said. I got to dress for work.

She handed me a mug. I nodded and watched her go, feeling kind of stuck in a little cage. I'd stayed in bigger motel rooms, you know? Didn't help that the kitchen had no windows and was overstuffed with stacks of bills and coupons and tin cans. The front door slammed, making me jump. Fever appeared in the doorway.

—Jeez, he said, seeing me, his eyes bugging.

I stood up, making sure I didn't hit my head on the ceiling lamp. He reached out and shook my hand. Then we stood there, staring. Fever didn't look nothing like Spade no more. He'd gotten a belly and grown a beard.

—Welcome back, he said finally. I'm going to take a shower.

—Okay, Fever. I'll just . . .

But he just turned and walked to the bathroom and closed the door. And I stood there, fighting the need to walk out. There wasn't nothing here I remembered. Everything had burned, except a little tiny photo hanging on the wall. One corner was blackened, but it was framed. It was from my first trip to Nana's, us all standing in front of her house. I stood there, looking at it real careful, rubbing my piece of Nana glass until Ma came back, dressed for work.

Us two sat in the kitchen with our coffees till Fever finished his shower. Then he sat across from us in his brown bathrobe. I smiled at him to keep from grinding my teeth.

—You lost a tooth, he said, rubbing his beard.

—In a fight, I told him. I been fighting for money.

—I heard, he said, getting up and pulling white bread out of a bag.

He bit off big bites. I was real hungry, but I didn't ask for none.

—Heard you made some cash, Fever said.

—Yeah. Lots. I only lost once.

—I heard, he said.

And I wanted to chuck him against the cabinets. Instead

I rubbed my neck and tilted my chair back on two legs. Ma'd been holding her breath and she let it out in a sentence:

—I got a new job, she said, then breathed in.

—Yeah? What kind of work? I asked her.

—Me? I'm cleaning. Your dad, he's working down by the dealership again with—

—How much money you got? Fever blurted.

He picked bread from between his teeth. I pulled out my pack of smokes. Ma got up and found an ashtray.

—I already told you: Lots.

—'Cause I got this idea, Fever said, sitting back down and pulling the pack out of my hand. We should use it for this one thing, this idea I got, right? I got it all figured out. See, this is what we're gonna do. . . . See, you and me, we're going to build a parking lot together. It'll be so easy.

He grabbed a bottle of rum and poured it in our coffees.

—Fever, how come you didn't talk to me at Nana's funeral?

—What? Oh, come on. Forget that. Listen to what I'm telling you.

I turned to Ma and asked:

—Did Spade call you while I was gone? He ever visit you two without me?

Ma sat silent, smoothing down the front of her blouse.

—WYATT! Listen to me here, Fever spat, patting my shoulder. Focus for a second on what I'm saying: I got the perfect plan. I even spotted the perfect empty lot. We'll just sit back and let the cash flow in with the cars, making us all rich, right?

—Give me a minute, I said, stabbing out my smoke.

The little rooms with all their junk squeezed me. I choked on that stink of strangers.

—Just give me a sec, I said, gulping the lukewarm coffee.

The two of them watched me stand and stumble into their hall and out their door. I raced down the stairs to the front of their building, sucking in clean night air. I'd never felt so lonely in my life. I growled through my teeth like a dog and punched the brick wall, the bite of grit in my knuckles feeling good. I couldn't think. Gosh, I wished I could remember how to use my brain like Gauge Coleman told me. I wished I remembered all the stuff Clark explained, but I couldn't. I wasn't smart enough. I couldn't just think up a plan like Spade or Fever. I could never think of nothing as smart as a parking lot, no way. I stomped up and down their sidewalk till the apartment building door swung open. Fever leaned out. He'd got dressed. His hair'd dried and was slicked back. He smiled a pinch-lipped smile and said:

—Your ma figured you'd just kept on walking.

—I was gonna, I said, trying not to cry.

—Come on. Let's walk to the corner for smokes. You ain't got none left.

So we walked to the gas station where I used to buy myself

ice-cream sandwiches. I hid my fists in my pockets, squeezing my piece of Nana glass tight in my right one, make-believing everything was gonna be okay, listening to Fever repeating how the parking lot would make us rich:

—We'll work together, okay? Plan it, buy it, open it together. We'll use some of your fight money, yeah? And maybe your ma can help a little. We'll get brand-new slick black asphalt paved in, have yellow lines painted on top. The lot's in the perfect spot, six blocks from the Coliseum, between a hardware store and taco shop. I bet we can get at least fourteen spots in there, maybe twenty regular-size cars. And we'll pack it for championship games. Jeez, Wyatt, you're big as a car. I bet you can measure the spots with your body. . . .

Fever laughed, patting my shoulder, holding the door open, and waiting for me outside, still chuckling when I got back.

CHAPTER THIRTY-FIVE

SO FEVER AND ME, WE

got that parking lot together. Planned it together. Bought it together. Opened it together. And I did use most of my left-over fight money. And Ma did help a little. We got brand-new asphalt and lines painted on top. Beautiful yellow lines. Fever, he made me measure the spots with my body, making like snow angels, and we got fourteen spots six blocks from the Coliseum. The perfect spot.

Today was the grand opening, and rain was coming down hard. And there I was, standing on the curb to avoid the flood-ing gutter, with Fever hollering at me from back by our new chain-link fence. I couldn't hear a word he was saying through the wind and the drops smacking my yellow slicker and the car jam honking and cheers from people running the six blocks to the Coliseum, waving pennants under umbrellas. And Fever's voice like barking.

I blinked, trying to get the rain off my eyelashes, so I could see what Fever was saying from way back by the one car we got parked. Ma sat inside. I could see her shadow through the windshield and knew she was watching me, a brown paper sack full of deviled ham sandwiches sitting on her lap. They were the first sandwiches she'd ever made me. I mean ever. That was a big deal, just like me and Fever working together was a big deal. Fever was so mad his head bobbed, making the earflaps on his hat wag. He looked pretty silly, but my pants being soaked down to my socks, cold and squishy, made nothing funny right then.

—WYATT! GOD DANG IT! GET THEM CARS IN HERE! WYATT!

I heard him that time, only he didn't say dang. He said the cussword. I still don't like nobody using them words at me, even if he's my dad. He didn't have to get that way with me. It wasn't my fault no one was turning in. It wasn't my fault they were first all driving past us to the Coliseum lot. I knew they'd see that sign flashing FULL-FULL-FULL and drive back around. I wouldn't have walked six blocks in that downpour neither. I was only out there 'cause I was the owner and I had to work. I had to wave a flashlight to make them notice me and my yellow slicker and the sign that said SIX BUCKS.

I wanted to tell him that nobody hollers at me no more. I wanted to holler back:

—WHAT DO YOU WANT ME TO DO, ANYWAY? JUMP ON THEIR HOODS? PUSH THEIR CARS IN HERE? STEAL THEIR WALLETS? HUH, FEVER? THAT WHAT YOU WANT? HUH?

I started to shake. The plastic flashlight dented in my grip. That's when I hollered into the street:

—SIX BUCKS! PARK HERE! SIX BUCKS!

And kept on till my throat hurt and I was drowning Fever out. I shivered, half from the cold and half from the madness I kept shoved deep down inside. My chest was like a overstuffed suitcase with my brain sitting on the lid. Fever yelled. Ma stared. The traffic noise screamed. The cold rain chomped on my skin. And that suitcase inside me bulged. And then a wailing started far off. The game was about to start. Air horns like emergency sirens surrounded me. My fists tightened. Pictures flashed inside my eyes. I was in the old house. I was so much smaller and skinnier, so lonely and scared. I remembered everything like comic strips flashing past. And then the suitcase in my chest burst open. My fists tightened, busting open the flashlight, big D batteries splashing into the rush of water at my feet. I spun toward Fever, wiping my eyes, so I could see again. Cheers reached us. The game had started. Fever's hollers jumped at me. I wished I didn't understand. You can handle this, I told myself. Calm down. Don't get so peeved. Be the bigger guy.

—YOU GODDAMNED STUPID KID! I SAID GET THEM IN HERE, YOU LAZY SHIT! and I felt his words in my overflowing chest.

—NO! I hollered back. YOU GET THEM CARS IN HERE! YOU! YOU!

I chucked the broke flashlight at him, but he was too far away and it clattered between us. Ma got out of the parked car, the sack of sandwiches falling onto the wet asphalt. She told me not to holler. I ignored her, kicking the puddle at my feet, shouting:

—YOU'RE LAZY, FEVER! then added, YOU IDIOT!

He stomped toward me, the broke flashlight crunching under his boot.

—Walt, don't, Ma told him, taking two steps and stopping.

—No, Bonnie, it's time this asshole learned.

I could see his name on her lips. She grabbed a hunk of her hair as her face twisted up. Fever kept coming, stomping slow.

—You waste of time—

—STOP! I spit.

And Fever stopped one step from being chest-to-chest with me, and he smirked. And that was it. That twist in his mouth said everything he'd ever yelled at me for my whole life and my fist connected straight into his face, covering that mouth and

226

those eyes and snapping his nose from my sight. It felt like my fist had gone through him, but he was down on the ground, hat knocked off and wide-eyed, scared I was going to do worse. He looked like a confused little kid with me the grown-up above him. I am grown up, you know, I am.

My arms fell to my sides. I never wanted to touch nobody again. Two old ladies at the bus stop across the street waddled over to see if Fever was okay. Blood dribbled out the corner of his lips. I watched the look in his eyes change to embarrassed. Ma ran to him, knelt down, and waved the old ladies back across the street.

I thought a lot of words.

Ma used her sleeve to clean up the blood and shook her head.

—FUCK! I shouted, and burst out laughing.

It surprised us all. Now Ma looked punched. I laughed so hard I choked and coughed, my head tilting back, up to the humungous dark sky. Then, looking down at them two strangers on the ground below me, I smirked. All the shreds of me had been scrambled till that one moment. I realized I am ugly and mean and nice and smart and dumb and good-looking. I am part my ma and Nana, part Lynnesha and Gauge Coleman and Clark Kent, part Uncle Spade and Fever and . . .

—I gotta go now, I said, and left them there on the ground.

The rain slowed to a mist and I took off my slicker, letting it flail in the wind. I wasn't so cold no more. I let go, watching the yellow plastic blow across the street. I breathed deep and walked away from the lot, the Coliseum, the City. On my own. *And I'm okay with that*, I thought for the first time. My white T-shirt slicked tight to my skin, too small, so I peeled it off. And I walked until I got tired, then I decided to catch this bus and ran into you. Think I'll sleep now. I'm tired of telling, of thinking so hard. And when I wake up, I'll try to figure all this out. And you know what? I'm okay with that.